CAIRO ROSE *and the* SWORD *of* DAMOCLES

Claude G. Luisada

Cairo Rose and the Sword of Damocles

Copyright © 2025 Claude G. Luisada

Produced and printed by Stillwater River Publications.
All rights reserved. Written and produced in the United States of America. This book may not be reproduced or sold in any form without the expressed, written permission of the author(s) and publisher.

Visit our website at
www.StillwaterPress.com
for more information.

First Stillwater River Publications Edition.

ISBN: 978-1-968548-06-3

1 2 3 4 5 6 7 8 9 10
Written by Claude G. Luisada.
Cover & interior book design by Matthew St. Jean.
Cover assets by Peter Hermes Furian (map), woverwolf (sword), and svetlanais (paper texture) / Adobe Stock.
Published by Stillwater River Publications,
West Warwick, RI, USA.

The views and opinions expressed in this book are solely those of the author(s) and do not necessarily reflect the views and opinions of the publisher.

This novel is dedicated to my stepson, Greg Nagle, and his wife, Barbara Lynn, with my heartfelt thanks for having made my last years so much more pleasant.

Cast of Characters

United States

David Knox – CIA Field Agent for the Middle East
Dean Morrison – CIA Deputy Director of Operations
Ernest Hilliard – Dir. of Middle East Operations
Jack Riley – Control for David Knox
President Eisenhower

Israel

Helga Horowitz – Field Agent aka “Cairo Rose”
Moshe Feingold – Dir. of Mossad – Israeli Intelligence Agency
Manny Epstein – Mossad Deputy Director of Middle East Operations
Esther Epstein – Wife of Manny
David Ben-Gurion – Prime Minister of Israel

Egypt

Gamal Abdel Nasser – President of Egypt
Shukaki Al-Qalli – President of Syria
Suleiman Nabulsi – Prime Minister of Jordan
Nazi SS Colonel Doctor Rudolph Schweitz – Nuclear Physicist
Nazi SS Colonel Doctor Siegfreid Reicher – Chemist and researcher in poison gases
Nazi SS Colonel Eric Rochman – Former Dir. of Treblinka Execution Camp, known as “Butcher of Treblinka”
Abdul – Grocery store owner
Alex – Chemist at labs
Omar – Physicist at labs

Prologue

November 1, 1944
Northeast of Warsaw, Poland
Treblinka Execution Camp

At the infamous Treblinka Execution Camp, the newly arrived prisoners, the majority Jewish, are quickly taken to the bare barracks. Within days, if not hours, most are executed in gas chambers. One such family is from Kyiv, Ukraine, a country that at the time was part of the Soviet Union, and that was invaded by German troops in 1941-42. This was the Horowitz family, who were Jewish. Paul, the father, was a noted surgeon. Marcia, his wife, a beautiful and talented woman, was a concert violinist well-known in Europe. They had two daughters: Helga, seventeen, and Sharon, eleven.

Marcia and the younger daughter were quickly separated from the rest of the family and, within two days, were dead. Helga was put into a forced labor unit. Paul, the father, attracted the attention of Colonel Rochman, the Director of Treblinka, often referred to as the "Butcher of Treblinka." This is a well-earned title, since in time Treblinka would become one of the most efficient and successful extermination camps, second only to the infamous Auschwitz death camp.

Paul Horowitz is put into a small, special cell. Colonel Rochman believes, mistakenly, that Horowitz may have valuable information that could benefit the Nazi war effort. He is tortured aggressively but remains silent. After a few days, Rochman loses patience and orders more intense torture. But before that torture can be applied, Paul Horowitz's heart gives out, and he expires quietly. No one paid attention. No one cared.

In another part of Treblinka, young Helga Horowitz, exhausted after seventeen hours of forced labor, huddled in the cold under a thin blanket. She was afraid and wondered if she would survive and if her family was still alive. No one paid attention. No one cared.

At seventeen years old, Helga is already a beautiful young woman with a well-developed figure. One day, Colonel Rochman noticed her and had her brought to his quarters. He raped her repeatedly and then tired of her and sent her back to hard labor.

A small group of prisoners, all working at hard labor, formed a plan to escape. On a dark moonless night, they managed to subdue two guards and to escape. During that first night, they hiked without stopping, hoping to get far enough away that no guards from Treblinka could find them. In the following days and weeks, they continued moving westwards until eventually they reached the neutral country of Turkey. There they hid for a time in a Catholic Church. The church's priest put them in touch with the Archbishop of Istanbul, who was sympathetic to Jews trying to escape the Nazi terror. He issued them false documents. In time, the entire group reached Palestine, at the time a British Protectorate. In 1948, a portion of Palestine became the Jewish state of Israel.

A few years later, Helga Horowitz, now an adult and a strikingly beautiful young woman, joined the Israeli Intelligence Service, the Mossad, and was given the code name "Cairo Rose."

Over a period of a few years, Helga completed a number of daring missions and became one of the Mossad's top agents.

But Helga had grown into a silent and bitter young woman, emotionally scarred by her treatment at the hands of Colonel Rochman, the loss of her entire family, and her escape from Treblinka.

1

Spring 1957
Cairo, Egypt
President Nasser's Villa

IN A SECLUDED AREA OF CAIRO, EGYPT, IS A LARGE LUXURIOUS mansion located in the center of a vast green lawn and surrounded by woods on all sides. A very tall wall protects the entire property. This was the sumptuous residence of President Gamal Abdel Nasser, the dictator of Egypt. It is constantly patrolled by heavily armed guards with attack dogs on leashes.

Within the walls of this mansion, a very high-level secret meeting took place. It was attended by President Nasser, the host, President al-Qalli, the President of Syria, and Prime Minister Suleiman Nabulsi, the newly elected Prime Minister of Jordan. Also in attendance were three former Nazi top-level officers. Two were scientists, and all three were SS officers. All were former members of the Nazi elite during World War II. They are: Colonel Doctor Rudolph Schweitz, a nuclear scientist; Colonel Doctor Seigfrid Reicher, an expert on poison gas; and Colonel Eric Rochman, who was the Commandant of the infamous Treblinka Execution Camp and was known as the "Butcher of Treblinka." All three men were fanatical Nazis, extremely anti-Semitic, and all were considered war criminals by the post-war Allied military tribunals. However, they managed to escape to Egypt in the late 1940s with the assistance of the Nazi escape organization known as the "Odessa." Now they had been summoned to this meeting by President Nasser, who hoped to utilize their scientific and security expertise.

President Nasser, as the host, chaired the meeting.

Nasser said, "President al-Qalli and Prime Minister Nabusi, I am truly grateful that you were able to attend this meeting. I believe that what is decided here today will be momentous in the annals of world history.

Let me first introduce these other three gentlemen. They are all former Colonels and members of the German Nazi Party. They are: Colonel Doctor Schweitz, a well-known nuclear scientist; Colonel Doctor Reicher, a noted chemist and expert in poison gases; and Colonel Rochman, formerly the Commandant of the Treblinka Execution Camp."

The three Nazis each nodded their head respectfully as they were introduced, but remained silent.

Nasser continued, "Gentlemen, it is my hope that, with the expertise of these two scientists plus the security directed by Colonel Rochman, we can, once and forever, destroy the State of Israel. If we accomplish that goal, the entire world will thank us, I have no doubt!"

Everyone present at the meeting applauded.

President Nasser continued, "I can put a considerable amount of funds into this project. However, I would be most grateful if Syria and Jordan could also contribute some funds. Say maybe fifteen percent from each of you?"

President al-Qalli said, "President Nasser, I think Syria will be proud to take part in this historic endeavor. You can count on us!"

Now, Prime Minister Nabulsi chimed in and said, "Yes,

indeed, President Nasser, Jordan will be equally proud to join you in this truly very important project!"

The three former Nazis present remained silent but looked very pleased at what was said.

President Nasser said, "Gentlemen, I am delighted at your responses. I propose that this project be called 'Sword of Damocles.' I recommend that we refer to it as simply 'SOD' as a measure of security. I have a great deal of confidence in these three gentlemen!" And Nasser pointed at the three Nazis.

Nasser continued, "I shall quickly move ahead and have an underground laboratory and manufacturing area built. I will keep you two allies updated as to our progress. Needless to say, there must be total secrecy as to what the 'Sword of Damocles' is and as to the ultimate goal."

President al Qualli of Syria said, "President Nasser, the success of this momentous project will make you famous in the history of mankind!"

Nasser glowed at the compliment.

Everyone present nodded and applauded, and sometime later the meeting broke up. The stage was now set for a momentous event.

The three Nazis now huddled together to begin the planning that would be necessary if the 'Sword of Damocles' project was to succeed.

Dr. Schweitz took the lead in this discussion. He was a small man with the features of a weasel and walked with a limp due to an injury sustained as a child. He was very intelligent and was close to perfecting a nuclear weapon in 1945, but was interrupted by the end of the war in Europe and the fall of the Nazi regime.

Dr. Reicher is quite tall and thin, with nondescript features. He was very successful during World War II in developing a variety of very effective poison gases. Unfortunately for the Nazis, they did not have the opportunity to use these gases.

Colonel Rochman is a big man with a thick neck. His face betrayed his total lack of empathy for human beings.

All three men were psychotic and extremely anti-Semitic. They were married and abandoned their wives in war-torn Germany in 1945, and treated women like slaves. In Egypt, the three Nazis kept a number of prostitutes always available.

Dr. Schweitz said, "I believe the three of us need to determine exactly how to destroy Israel. Based on that, we need to plan on how much space we'll need in the underground labs and manufacturing area and how many technicians will be required so that we can inform President Nasser."

Dr. Reicher said, "Absolutely! And we need to get busy to figure all of that out quickly!"

The three men began working together to do all of the necessary planning. Schweitz put forward the basic idea that the best way to destroy Israel was by striking with hundreds of short-range missiles that had nuclear warheads, plus other missiles that would spread poison gas. The others agreed enthusiastically. The plan was put before President Nasser, and after some consideration, he also agreed. The underground building that was to be built would be based on that plan.

The 'Sword of Damocles' project was now underway. Could anything stop the destruction of Israel?

2

May 6, 1957
Jerusalem, Israel
Mossad Headquarters

In Jerusalem there is a medium-sized office building distinguished by having few windows. This building is the headquarters of the Mossad, the Israeli intelligence agency. In a top-floor meeting room, a meeting was about to take place. Two men sat in the room waiting for a third person. One man was Moshe Feingold, the Director of Mossad. The other was Manny Epstein, the Director for Mossad Middle East Operations. The two men sat quietly, each lost in his thoughts.

A knock sounded on the door, which was immediately opened. A woman entered. She was on the tall side, with a voluptuous figure and a gorgeous face. Wherever she went, she showed a presence.

She was greeted warmly by the two men as she sat down at the conference table. This was Helga Horowitz, Mossad code name "Cairo Rose," a top agent for the Mossad. She appeared to be in her late twenties. Director Feingold, as he often did, immediately began speaking.

He said, "Helga, thank you for coming here to this meeting on short notice, but I believe there is good reason. We have received some very disturbing news from one of our agents in Cairo. It seems that some weeks ago, three former Nazi Colonels very quietly slipped into Egypt. We know who they are and have dossiers on all three. It appears that in May 1945, after the collapse of the Nazi regime, they managed to slip unnoticed to a small town in Austria. Despite being on the Allied War Criminal List, they evaded capture for a number of years. Then we believe they managed to slip into Italy, the port of Genoa to be precise, and a small freighter that brought them to Alexandria, Egypt. We know of the organization that helped them all along. Now there is a rumor that these three Nazis have been meeting with President Nasser, the leader of Egypt. Prime Minister Ben-Gurion is very concerned as to what these three Nazis might be plotting against Israel, particularly since they are known to be fanatics and extremely anti-semitic. In fact, the Prime Minister is so concerned that he consulted with the American President, Dwight Eisenhower, about what the potential danger represented by these three. President Eisenhower not only agreed but, after he talked to the CIA, the U.S. intelligence agency, decided that a CIA agent familiar with the Middle East should come to Israel and work together with a Mossad agent."

At this point, Feingold stopped talking so as to organize what he was going to say next. Then he began speaking again, but in a somewhat tone of voice.

"Helga, you are possibly our best agent that we have when it comes to penetrating Egypt and getting information. But there is a problem. Two of these Nazis are scientists, but the third is the former Commander of the Treblinka Death Camp, the place where you were imprisoned, where you lost your entire family, and from which you eventually escaped. Yes, I am referring to Colonel Eric Rochman. So you see, Helga, while the Mossad would like to have you infiltrate Egypt once again, we are very concerned as to how the presence of this Colonel Rochman might affect your judgment and your ability to perform what may turn out to be the most difficult assignment you have ever been given."

Feingold stopped talking, and he and Epstein waited to see what Helga Horowitz's reaction would be. Helga had been listening to all of this intently without saying a word. Now she looked down at the conference table, obviously considering what she had just been told. Finally, she looked up and, with a resolute tone of voice, responded:

"Gentlemen, I appreciate the confidence you have shown in me, and I understand why you are concerned about my possible reaction to having Rochman involved. I honestly believe I can remain objective if I undertake this mission. Furthermore, if I have to work together with a CIA agent, then I would think he or she could monitor what I am doing and warn me that I am no longer being objective."

Feingold looked at Epstein with raised eyebrows as if to say, "What do you think?"

Manny Epstein thought about it briefly and said, "Mr. Director, I really believe that we can have total confidence in Helga." Feingold said, "All right, Helga, I guess you rate this assignment. As soon as the CIA agent arrives, we will brief both of you on what little information we have as of now. Helga, thank you for coming and for your response."

Helga thanked the two Directors and, without another word, quietly left the meeting room.

May 10, 1957
Georgetown, Washington, D.C., USA
A Small Condominium

David Knox rolled over in his bed, took a look at his alarm clock, and decided it was probably time to get up. David was a muscular, six-foot-tall man with sandy hair. He had a pleasant face, and when he smiled, his face lit up. He had gray eyes that were not particularly noticeable, except if he was truly angry or upset. Then he had a habit of looking at people in a manner that could freeze them in their tracks.

David was a Central Intelligence Agency (CIA) field agent. Born in Brookline, Massachusetts, a suburb of Boston, he had lost his parents in a car crash at an early age and was raised by very loving maternal grandparents who legally adopted him. His grandmother was Jewish, but David was never told that. He attended Harvard University and graduated with a BS in Political Science and with a minor in psychology. He also ran the mile on the track team and rowed a single scull racing boat. After graduating, he spent four years in the U.S. Air Force, where he trained to become a pilot. In the Air Force, he flew Lockheed C-130 Hercules attack transports. When he left the Air Force, he was recruited by the CIA. Now, at age thirty-two, he had six years of field experience with the CIA and was considered one of their most experienced field agents. David was still single, which was pretty normal for field agents who were away from home a great deal of the time.

David had recently returned from a three-month assignment in the Middle East and was looking forward to a minimum of a couple of weeks of rest.

Now, as he padded around his small condo getting dressed, he was debating what to do after breakfast when his phone rang.

David walked over to his desk, frowning. He could not think of anyone calling him since he had recently returned from overseas on a long assignment. He picked up the phone and said hello.

"Hello, David, Dean Morrison here. Sorry to bother you, I know you just came back from a long assignment. Something has just come up. Could you please come to Langley this morning?"

David knew that if Morrison, the CIA Deputy Director for Field Operations, requested his presence, it was the same as an order. Furthermore, it sounded as if something important had come up.

David said, "Of course, Mr. Morrison, at what time do you want me there?"

Morrison said, "David, can you get here fairly quickly?"

David responded, "Yes, sir. I'll try to be there within the hour."

Morrison said, "David, come directly to my office. See you then," and he hung up.

David quickly shaved, got dressed in slacks, a short-sleeved shirt, a sport jacket, and loafers. He got into his five-year-old sports car and headed for the CIA Headquarters located in Langley, northern Virginia.

Same Day, 10 a.m.
Langley, Virginia
CIA Headquarters

David passed through the security controls without delay and headed for the top-floor office of Morrison. Morrison's secretary, who knew him well, simply waved him in. David entered the office and saw that, in addition to Morrison, there were two other men present. One was Ernest Hilliard, Director of Middle East Operations, and the other was Jack Riley, David's handler. The three men all stood as David entered the office and greeted him warmly. They all respected Knox highly. Morrison waved David to a chair and pointed to a coffee pot and some sweet rolls, guessing that David had not had time for breakfast. Then Morrison began talking.

"David, we had some very disturbing news yesterday from the Mossad, the Israeli Intelligence Agency. Somehow, they have learned that a few days ago a secret meeting took place in Cairo. Present at the meeting were President Nasser, the President of Syria, the Prime Minister of Jordan, plus three very unsavory former Nazy Colonels about whom the Agency knows quite a bit. Neither the Mossad nor the Agency knows what the meeting covered, but considering who attended the meeting, it has caused a great deal of concern in Jerusalem. The Mossad contacted the Agency and asked for one of our top agents to fly to Israel together with Hilliard, whom you know quite well. The Mossad has an agent in mind who would work together with you. The CIA knows very little about this agent except that her code name is "Cairo Rose" and she has completed a number of very successful missions on behalf of the Mossad."

David raised a hand to politely interrupt Morrison and said, "Sir, when I've been in the Middle East, I have heard the name 'Cairo Rose' mentioned. She appears to be quite feared by some of those governments!"

Morrison said, "Hm, that is interesting. At any rate, that is the assignment. David, we all know that you need a break from overseas operations, but when we tell you who the three Nazis that attended that very high-level meeting were, I believe you'll understand why there is all this concern. In fact, I can tell you that the Israeli Prime Minister himself has communicated with President Eisenhower and passed on his own very serious concern, but that is for your ears only!"

David said nothing, merely nodded, and waited patiently for what was going to come next in what was obviously a briefing meant specifically for him. Ernest Hilliard picked up the trail of the briefing.

Hilliard said, "David, the three Nazi Colonels were all three high on the list of war criminals that the Allied Governments are still hoping to bring to justice. They managed to escape to Egypt and are now working directly for President Nasser. They are Colonel Doctor Rudolph Scheitz, a physicist who specialized in nuclear research, Colonel Doctor Siegfried Reicher, a chemist who directed the creation of new poison gases, and Colonel Erik Rochman, the former Director of the Treblinka Execution Camp who was known as the "Butcher of Treblinka" All three of these men were in the SS, and all three are known to be extremely anti-Semitic. So you see, David, the Mossad believes something is brewing there in Egypt, and with these three former SS officers involved, it could be something very nasty indeed!"

David again nodded. He knew from experience there had to be more to the briefing. Now Jack Riley took up the briefing. He and David knew each other well and had actually become friends.

Riley said, "David, we don't know exactly how the Mossad got their initial information about this meeting, but in the past, their intelligence has been extremely reliable. The fact that the Israeli Prime Minister himself contacted the President is certainly an indication of the Israelis' very real concern. They are not usually in the habit of coming to us for help in the area of intelligence.

However, David, the Agency does not feel it can just order you to go to Israel and get involved in what may turn out to be a long and difficult mission. There is no question that you need a break after your long overseas activity. We have all agreed that if you do accept this assignment, it will be only if you volunteer to do so. So you need to think about it!"

David was silent for a full three minutes, looking down at the conference table. No one said a word out of respect for him and realizing he was attempting to make a decision.

Finally, David looked up and met the glances of the others.

Then he said, "I'll take the assignment. It sounds pretty challenging!"

Morrison exclaimed, "Good for you, David! The Agency really appreciates your attitude!"

Riley picked up the briefing and said, "What is going to happen next is that Hilliard, you, and I are flying to Israel to meet with the Mossad. We leave this evening on TWA. Hopefully, when we meet with the Mossad, we'll have a better picture of what exactly this is all about. So, David, you'd better get back home and pack. A car will pick you up this afternoon at three. Any questions at this time, David?"

David shrugged and said, "Guess I'll have to wait and see what happens next."

Morrison said, "David, I want you to know that the Agency really appreciates your making yourself available on such short notice, particularly after just coming back from a long assignment. But we would not have called on you again so soon unless there were strong indications that something very important was happening in the Middle East. While we have other field agents with Middle East experience, you were available, and you have an excellent past record. That is why you were chosen to go to Israel. Good luck to you!"

David thanked Morrison and quickly left the building. As he drove home, he found himself thinking some more about the upcoming assignment. It seemed to him that the entire project had been put together in a great hurry and with very little hard information. He hoped that in the next few days there would be more information available. David had worked with the Mossad before and had found their agents to be very tough, yet reliable and professional.

Same Day, 7:00 p.m.
New York City, USA
New York Idlewild International Airport

KNOX AND THE OTHER two CIA agents waited patiently to board their TWA non-stop flight to Tel Aviv, Israel. They had flown in from Washington and had arrived ninety minutes earlier. Traveling with diplomatic passports, they were ushered aboard the TWA flight ahead of the other passengers and led to their first-class seats. David, as a former U.S. Air Force pilot and holder of a private pilot license, still maintained an active interest in aviation. He had flown on TWA Lockheed Constellations frequently as he crossed the North Atlantic to and from his assignments. Now, as he looked idly out the window, he suddenly realized there was something different about this aircraft. And then it hit him. This Constellation had a different wing than all the previous Constellations that he had traveled on. The wing was much longer and slimmer, and the reciprocating engines were located further out from the fuselage. David remembered reading about the latest aircraft design to come from Lockheed. It was called the Jetstream Model 1649A and boasted a very long range and a much quieter cabin interior.

Now, as he settled in for the long flight ahead, David planned on a good sleep once dinner was finished.

He heard the first of the four big Curtiss Wright 29-cylinder Turbo-Compound engines coming to life. David was always impressed by the way those engines started. The propeller would begin to revolve very slowly, then as the cylinders began to ignite, great gobs of gray smoke would be ejected, the rumbling increased, and finally the engine would be operating at low speed.

Shortly, the aircraft began taxiing to the runway. After a short delay, the big Connie moved to the head of the runway, take-off power was applied, and the plane began to roll. After a long take-off, it lifted off and turned northeast.

David and his two companions could not converse easily, and so they all sat quietly, lost in their individual thoughts as the Connie climbed to its operating altitude of 23,000 feet. Dinner was served, and afterwards the cabin lights were dimmed. David noticed with pleasure that the cabin was in fact quieter than on other transports, and reclining his seat and pulling a blanket over himself quickly fell asleep.

May 11, 1957, 1:00 p.m.
In Flight

David woke up to find that they were flying over what he was pretty sure was Ireland. Soon breakfast was served. The attractive cabin stewardess seemed to give David a little bit of extra attention. David eventually noticed this, but knew this was not a time or place to try to be overly friendly with the stewardess. He smiled at her politely and did nothing more. Jack Riley, who was sitting next to David, leaned over and said in a low voice, "David, I do believe that attractive stewardess is showing an interest in you."

David looked at his friend Riley, shrugged, and said, "I don't think I'm going to have a chance to get to know her better. Duty calls, unfortunately."

Riley laughed and said nothing more.

The flight passed over England, France, Switzerland, and Italy, and then began the crossing of the Mediterranean Sea. The new model of the Lockheed Constellation had a range that enabled non-stop flights from New York to Israel. An hour out from Tel Aviv, a snack was served, and then the flight crew began the descent for the landing at Tel Aviv's Ben Gurion International Airport.

After landing, the three agents were hustled through Customs and Passport Control to where a government car awaited them, which took them to Jerusalem and their hotel.

After dinner, the three men retired to their individual rooms, knowing that early the next morning they would be meeting with their Mossad counterparts.

May 12, 1957
Jerusalem, Israel
Mossad Intelligence Agency Headquarters

Early the next morning, the three CIA agents were driven to the Mossad Headquarters, a nondescript five-story building located in the business section of New Jerusalem. The building was distinctive only because it had far fewer windows than typical office buildings. David guessed that such a feature was deliberately designed in the building to prevent enemy agents from listening to conversations by means of sophisticated listening devices that could pick up conversations through glass windows.

The three CIA agents were escorted to a top-floor conference room where two men and a woman were waiting. The men were Moshe Feingold, Director of Mossad, and Manny Epstein, Mossad Deputy Director for Middle East Operations. The woman was Helga Horowitz, a Mossad agent, whose code name was "Cairo Rose." They all stood up as the CIA agents walked in. One of the Israelis stepped forward, introduced himself with a warm, welcoming smile, and said, "Shalom, gentlemen. I am Moshe Feingold, Director of Mossad. It is truly a pleasure and an honor to welcome all of you to Israel. Let me introduce you around."

Moshe Feingold was a pleasant-looking middle-aged individual with the manner of a university professor. Manny Epstein was taller, thinner, and looked older than Finegold. Helga Horowitz appeared to be in her mid or late twenties. She was tall and extremely attractive. She had long, slim legs and large, firm breasts. When David was introduced to her and they shook hands, he discovered she had a very firm grip but no smile on her face. In fact, her face showed no emotion whatsoever.

With the introductions out of the way, everyone sat down.

Feingold offered coffee and breakfast rolls to everyone and then began the meeting.

Feigned said, "Gentlemen, I want to pass on to you the little we know about what appears to be a very nasty business. We received a written communication from an unknown person in Egypt. He or she seems to have some inside information. Mossad has already been able to confirm part of the message. It seems that some days ago, there was a secret meeting of President Nasser of Egypt, together with the President of Syria and the Prime Minister of Jordan. Also supposedly in attendance were three former high-level Nazi individuals, two scientists, and a former director of an execution camp. They are all high on the list of war criminals that the Allied powers have been searching for since the end of World War II. One was a nuclear scientist, one was a chemist expert in poison gases, and the third was a brutal SS killer. The Mossad has dossiers on all three of these men. We have been told that President Nasser has concocted some kind of plan called the 'Sword of Damocles.' But that's all we know. Considering who is involved, the State of Israel is taking this whole thing very seriously! I only wish I had more hard information to pass on to you."

Morrison said, "Director, I think the CIA can agree with you that whatever this plan of Nasser entails, it is likely to be very dangerous. The question now seems to be: how should we proceed and where does the CIA fit in?"

During this part of the meeting, David had been sitting quietly, not saying a word. He had previously met both Feingold and Epstein and considered them to be highly professional intelligence agents. But David did not know what to make of Helga Horowitz. She was an exceptionally stunning woman with slightly Oriental features, a voluptuous figure, and brilliant blue eyes that shone like diamonds. She was wearing shorts which revealed her slim, beautiful legs. But her face betrayed absolutely no emotion, and it made David somewhat uncomfortable. He had difficulty not staring at Helga because of her beauty, but finally managed to concentrate on what was being said instead. Now, David decided it was time for him to speak up.

He said, "Gentlemen and Miss Horowitz, I am not quite clear on what my role here is going to be, but if I am to be an active participant, then maybe the next step is for myself and Miss Horowitz to meet and attempt to lay out some plan of action. But I really do not know if that is what you all had in mind?"

Feingold said, "Mr. Knox, that is precisely what we of the Mossad had in mind. Director Morrison, what is your view?"

Morrison said, "Yes, it would seem that putting the experience of David and Helga together could result in an excellent team effort. Miss Horowitz, what do you think?"

Helga merely shrugged and said nothing.

Manny Epstein chimed in, "Gentlemen, Helga has been in the habit of working alone. However, if David and Helga could work together smoothly, then I agree they absolutely should. After all, they both bring different but important operational experience to this effort. Working together could well result in a quicker and better resolution of this whole problem. That fact may turn out to be that at some point their working together as a team could be a factor if we are to avoid what otherwise might turn out to be a disaster for Israel!"

Feingold said, "It seems that we all agree that David and Helga should work together and that the sooner they begin that process, the better. I can promise that the facilities and employees of the Mossad and of Israel will be put at their disposal."

Morrison said, "Absolutely! I can also promise the wholehearted co-operation of the CIA. President Eisenhower has made this project a priority."

Feingold said, "I think that settles it. Let's have David and Helga begin working immediately. Good luck to you both!"

Morrison said, "David, Riley and I are flying back to the States this afternoon, so I'll be saying goodbye. I know I am leaving you in good hands."

David said goodbye to Morrison and Riley, and they left to catch their flight back to the U.S.

There were some last-minute remarks, and then the meeting broke up, leaving David and Helga alone in the conference room. David looked at Helga and asked, "Do we work here or in some other office?"

Helga replied, "I have a small office on a different floor. Follow me."

With that, Helga stood up and led David to a lower floor and to a small office with a table, two chairs, and a telephone.

They sat down, and David asked, "Do you mind if I call you Helga?"

Helga said, "No, of course not. Where do you think we should start?"

David said, "Right now, I am staying in a hotel. Do you happen to know if any arrangement has been made as to where I should live while I am in Jerusalem?"

Helga said, "As it happens, an arrangement has been made. I live in an apartment building near here that is used exclusively by government employees. They have small apartments, and there is a communal dining room on the ground floor. I should think that would be adequate."

David said, "I'm sure that would be fine. If you show me where this building is, then I'd like to move my luggage from the hotel. Also, I had to skip breakfast, so maybe I can eat a quick lunch and then we can get to work this afternoon."

Helga said, "I have my car here. I'll run you to your hotel and then to the new apartment. We can eat lunch there and then come back here."

And that is what they did.

After David moved his luggage to the small apartment in the government employee building, he and Helga went to the communal dining room, where David found the food to be quite good. During lunch, he tried to start a conversation with Helga but found that she was basically unresponsive. The meal was a quiet one, and David made no further attempt at having a casual conversation with Helga. He had the strange feeling that basically she was ignoring him, although he did not understand why that was.

Same Day, 2:00 p.m.
Jerusalem, Israel
Mossad Headquarters

DAVID AND HELGA got to work in the small office that she normally used by herself.

David said, "How should we begin, Helga? I know that I have a lot of questions and no answers."

Helga responded, "I feel pretty much the same way at this point. Why don't we start by you asking your questions?"

David said, "Fine. Let me ask you, do we have any idea who the person is that gave us an initial clue as to this plot of Nasser's?"

Helga replied, "No, no one in the Mossad has any idea who sent that message. We may have to wait until that person decides to give us more information."

David said, "O.K. But that sure doesn't give us much to go on. Helga, does the Mossad have some agents in Egypt who might pick up some clues or some information?"

Helga responded, "Yes, the Mossad does have agents there as well as possibly some other contacts. Let me go to another office and have the word go out to our agents in Egypt to start searching for any available information."

With that, Helga walked out of the office. When she returned a few minutes later, she informed David that the word would go out shortly.

David said, "Helga, as of right now, I don't see any way to do much. Maybe we need to be patient and see if we get more information in the meantime. I think that for today, we have done all we can. Let us meet tomorrow morning at say 9 a.m. Would that work for you? And in the meantime, if I go back to the apartment, I can unpack and get settled."

Helga agreed. She said, "I'll get you back to your apartment and then later on I'll take you to the dining room again so that I can show you how that works in the evening."

David said, "That would be great! Thank you."

The two agents left the building and walked to their common residence, which was not very far away.

3

May 13, 1957
Jerusalem, Israel
Mossad Headquarters

DAVID AND HELGA WALKED TOGETHER TO THE MOSSAD Headquarters and immediately went to Helga's office. David found a message there that Moshe Feingold, the Mossad Director, wished to see him. David went to Feingold's office and was shown in by his secretary. Feingold greeted David, waved him to a chair, and got right down to business.

Feingold said, "David, I suspect that you may have already noticed that Helga is very withdrawn and shows little if any emotion. I felt that if the two of you were going to work closely together, you should know something of her background. She came from an upper-middle-class family that lived in Kiev, Ukraine, before the war. Her father was a successful surgeon, and her mother was a well-known concert violinist. Helga had a normal childhood and showed early in life that she was very intelligent. After the Germans occupied Ukraine in 1942, the family managed to avoid being sent to a concentration camp because her father had numerous high-ranking Nazis among his patients. In early 1944, however, when the Nazis implemented what became known as the "Final Solution," Helga's parents,

Helga, and her sister were all arrested and sent to the Treblinka Execution Camp. There, the parents were quickly exterminated. Helga and her sister were put to work in a slave work group, but her sister got sick and died. Helga survived but was raped repeatedly by Colonel Rochman, the Director of Treblinka. What she went through at Treblinka scarred her emotionally for life. It was a terrible time for her. Eventually, she and some of the other prisoners managed to escape and, over a period of months, made their way to Turkey, where the Catholic Church, using forged documents, got them to what was then known as Palestine. Helga lived in a kibbutz for some time, got a university education, and eventually joined the Mossad. Helga is fluent in Hebrew, English, Arabic, plus her native language, Ukrainian.

"I thought you should also know that Helga is very tenacious and tough. But she has a great deal of difficulty relating to people. What she went through during the war has left her isolated from those around her, and I suspect that her toughness is a cover because, in reality, she is emotionally fragile.

"So you see, David, I thought it might be important if you knew something of her background and her past."

David said nothing for a few seconds, merely looking off in the distance with a thoughtful expression on his face. Finally, he turned to Feingold and said, "Director, thank you very much for this information. I think it will help me have a much better working relationship with Helga and hopefully help the two of us get to the bottom of this 'Sword of Damocles' plot."

David again thanked the Director and went back to Helga's office. Helga did not ask him what the meeting with the Director had been about, but instead immediately brought up another subject.

Helga said, "We got another message from that unknown source. The message said that an industrial plant that is to look like a cotton textile mill is being built, located somewhere between Cairo and Alexandria. The mill is a fake. Underground, below the mill, there will be laboratories and manufacturing facilities. David, I think this may be the break we needed to move ahead with destroying this 'Sword of Damocles' before it can strike Israel!"

David nodded and said, "It would certainly seem so. But don't you think we need to discuss this with Manny Epstein before we make too many plans?"

Helga thought for a few seconds, then nodded her agreement.

She said, "Yes, you're right, David. Let me make an appointment for us to meet with Manny."

Same Day
Mossad Headquarters
Manny Epstein's Office

LATER THAT DAY, David and Helga entered Manny Epstein's office and were welcomed.

Manny said, "I imagine that you two are here because of the last message from our mysterious informant."

Helga said, "Yes, you're right. David and I are still not sure how to proceed. We thought you might be able to give us some direction."

Manny said, "As it happens, your timing is perfect. Feingold called me earlier. Let us all go and meet with him."

The three went to Feingold's office and sat down.

Feingold said, "I imagine you two are trying to figure out how to proceed after that last message that came yesterday. Well, the Prime Minister called this morning and we now have a rough idea of how to move forward. The Prime Minister believes that, while we could destroy this new facility in the near future while it's under construction, that would be meaningless. Nasser could simply build another facility somewhere else, possibly in a location much further south, a location where it might be very difficult for us to reach. The Prime Minister feels we have to be patient and let the construction proceed. In the meantime, we need to have a plan for keeping the 'Sword of Damocles' under surveillance. You should also know that the message from our secret informer said that this would be their last message. They indicated it was getting too dangerous for them, whoever they are, to send any more messages to the Mossad. So you can see what is really important is for Israel to gather as much information as possible without making anyone in Egypt realize they are under surveillance. That is what we need from you two right now. To accomplish that, it is likely that it will be necessary to insert you into Egypt at some point. So, you might begin planning along those lines."

Both agents nodded to show their agreement and returned to Helga's office with some definite goals for them to work toward.

Same Day
Jerusalem, Israel
Mossad Headquarters

BACK AT HELGA'S OFFICE, she said, "David, one thing that might be worth thinking about is how to enter Egypt and try to pinpoint the exact location of this fake textile mill. There is a way to go in at night with an Israeli patrol boat, putting us ashore on a beach. But if we go that way, we would be a long way from Cairo with no transportation. There is another way that the Mossad uses to get into Egypt. It requires the two of us to first fly to Tunis, Tunisia, using our real passports, and then fly on to Cairo on false passports. In Cairo, the Mossad owns a small apartment in a middle-income residential area that is available to us. There is also a car kept there that we can use. We could drive to the general area where the 'Sword of Damocles' is supposed to be building their facility, and maybe we can pinpoint the location. What do you think?"

David agreed and then asked, "How did the Mossad manage to own an apartment and have a car in Cairo?"

Helga explained, "The Mossad discovered an Egyptian landlord who absolutely hates the Nasser government. He was more than willing to sell the apartment to us as well as allow us to keep a car in a garage next to the building."

Helga said she would get the proper Mossad department to create false passports for them both, as well as make the airline reservations, and then left the office.

David was left alone with his thoughts. After receiving the briefing on Helga's past, he now thought of her with greatly increased respect. His university studies in psychology gave David a much better understanding of Helga's personality and explained why she seemed so withdrawn.

He suddenly realized that he and Helga had already fallen into a kind of daily pattern. They met for breakfast in the communal dining room, and then they walked to the Mossad Headquarters building. At lunchtime, they would go to one of a number of nearby little restaurants for a simple lunch before returning to the Mossad Headquarters. Then, in the late afternoon, they would walk together back to the building where each had a small apartment, have dinner together in the communal dining room, and then bid each other good night. Unfortunately, their meals together were always very quiet, and David made no real effort to break through Helga's wall of silence.

4

May 15, 1957
Tel Aviv, Israel
Ben Gurion International Airport

DAVID AND HELGA BOARDED THE TWA FLIGHT FOR TUNIS, Tunisia. They were traveling each on their individual diplomatic passport. They sat separately for security reasons and pretended to be strangers. The flight was direct to Tunis and flew over the blue Mediterranean Sea in bright sunlight. Reaching Tunis, they disembarked, entered the terminal, and very unobtrusively switched from their diplomatic passports to their fake U.S. passports, which showed them to be an American married couple who had just flown in from the U.S. They were also carrying fake documents that indicated that they were both amateur archeologists.

Four hours later, they embarked on the TWA flight that took them to Cairo. David happened to have a window seat, with Helga seated directly behind him. The flight departed Tunis, and the TWA Constellation climbed to a 9,500-foot cruise altitude. The flight followed the North African coastline on a brilliant, clear sunny day. As David looked down on the mostly barren coastline, his thoughts turned to World War II and the fighting between the British 8th Army and the German Afrika Corps led by the well-known General Erwin Rommel.

As the Constellation flew along, David relived in his mind what he remembered reading about the North African Campaign and the back-and-forth of the Allied and Axis armies.

After a relatively short flight, the Constellation began its descent, and shortly, they landed at Cairo International Airport. David and Helga, now walking together, since their fake passports indicated they were a married couple, passed through Passport Control and Customs without any difficulty. Then they took a taxi to the Mossad apartment. Somewhat tired from their all-day traveling, they unpacked, went out for an evening meal nearby, and then retired to the apartment and their individual bedrooms.

May 16, 1957
Cairo, Egypt
Area of Fake Textile Mill

After breakfast, David and Helga got into the small car the Mossad kept there and headed north in the general direction of the port city of Alexandria. They knew from the secret informant they had received that the facility being built to house the 'Sword of Damocles' project was somewhere in the general area between Alexandria and Cairo. They took the road to Alexandria, and after an hour of driving slowly, they came to a turn-off and noticed that numerous dump trucks were using the side road. Curious, they followed the road for around five miles and suddenly were stopped by a high fence and a guarded entrance. Before they knew it, they were surrounded by armed guards and told to exit their car. They pretended not to understand the Arabic being spoken, but followed the hand gestures and got out of their car. David addressed a sentry who appeared to be in charge.

The sentry said something in Arabic, and David, who did speak the language, pretended not to understand. He said, "We are American archeologists on an approved visit. Did we take the wrong road?"

The sentry asked in heavily accented English to see their passports, then told them, in no uncertain terms, to turn around and go back to the main highway. David thanked him profusely, acting the part of a rather confused visitor. The two agents got into their car and quickly left the area.

As they drove back to Cairo, David said, "Whew, that was a mean-looking bunch of guards. That checkpoint probably gets at least one lost car each day, which was a good thing for us. But I don't think we should go anywhere near that checkpoint again because they might remember us, and that could mean real trouble!"

Helga quietly agreed. On the way back to Cairo, Helga marked the approximate spot of the checkpoint on the highway map they had brought with them.

Back at their apartment, David and Helga were unsure what to do next. They discussed various possibilities. Finally, Helga said, "David, maybe we could drive to where the road map shows there is a small village not far from where we believe the fake mill is being built. If we have lunch there, we might gather some useful information. What do you think?"

David thought about it and then said, "That's an excellent idea, Helga. Yes, let's do that and see if we pick up any useful info."

David and Helga drove to a small village north of Cairo, where, if they were lucky, they might gather useful information relating in some way to the 'Sword of Damocles' project.

Arriving at the village, David and Helga parked their car

and then sauntered around pretending to be tourists. They visited various stores, hoping to find some connections to the fake mill under construction. In a small grocery store where they bought some fruit, they discovered that the owner spoke excellent English. They had a guarded conversation that gradually became more friendly and personal. Eventually, the owner revealed that he hated the Nasser regime. Then it came out that three men often visited the village, and they were all German and possibly Nazis. The owner further revealed that he had a deep hatred for any Nazi.

At that point, David and Helga gave the owner their first names, and he, in turn, told them his first name was Abdul. Since shoppers were beginning to come into the store, David and Helga left, but not before telling Abdul they would return sometime in the future.

On the drive back to Cairo, the two agents agreed that Abdul was worth cultivating on future visits.

Back in their apartment, Helga said, "David, I think that for the time being we might as well go back to Jerusalem. What do you think?"

David agreed, and Helga made airline reservations for their return to Israel the following day.

May 17, 1957
Jerusalem, Israel
Mossad Residence

THE FOLLOWING DAY, they flew back to Israel using the same indirect routing via Tunis and two different passports for each of them.

That evening in the communal dining room, David said, "Helga, I had an idea. I could rent a small plane, and we could fly offshore of Egypt and try to pinpoint exactly where the fake mill is located. If we fly fairly high, it might be possible to spot the site from a few miles offshore."

Helga was dubious about David's plan. She said, "If we are close enough to the shore to spot the mill, it might trigger the Egyptian radar, and their Air Force might send a jet fighter to either shoot us down or else force us to land. You never know with these people."

David responded, "If I filed an IFR flight plan that showed we were flying from Lebanon to Tobruk, Libya, that should protect us."

Helga asked, "What's an IFR flight plan?"

David smiled at the question and then explained, "An IFR flight plan means you are flying under Instrument Flight Rules. That's what airline flights use, and so do many small business aircraft. The flight plan could show that we took off from Beirut, Lebanon. But to do that, we would first fly near the Lebanese border without a flight plan, and we'd fly quite low. Then we would climb and pretend we had just departed from Beirut. Of course, the Israeli Air Force would have to be forewarned of our plan. Then, when we are near Lebanon, I would use the radio and file my IFR flight plan. Then we would start climbing and begin to fly out over water toward Libya. At some point, Egyptian radar would spot us and assume that we had departed from Beirut, Lebanon. It's that simple."

Helga looked dubious but finally agreed it might be worth a try.

Helga said, "We need to clear the entire plan with the Mossad. And by the way, David, I believe the Mossad keeps a number of small aircraft somewhere."

David said, "That's good to know. It's probably much better to use an aircraft that the Mossad regularly uses."

May 18, 1957
Jerusalem, Israel
Mossad Headquarters

THAT MORNING, the two agents went to the Mossad HQ and met with Manny Epstein. Helga submitted David's plan for flying across to Tobruk, Libya, where there was a small airport of adequate size to handle any general aviation aircraft. Later that day, Manny Epstein asked David and Helga to come to his office, and they promptly complied with the request. Once there, Epstein explained the reason for his request to visit him.

Epstein said, "David and Helga, flying to Tobruk might work. But there have been problems with landing in Libya. The part of your plan for flying near Beirut makes good sense. But from Beirut you could also fly directly to Cairo. It's half the distance and might enable you to fly quite close to the site that we suspect is where the fake mill we call the labs will be located. As far as landing in Cairo is concerned, we have done just that in recent months. As long as all you do is land and take on fuel, the Egyptians seem happy to take anyone's money. Also, there is a lot of air traffic at Cairo International Airport, including a fair number of business aircraft. So you should not stand out. Yes, flying over Egypt and landing in Cairo could be very risky. On the other hand, time is slipping by, and we really need some confirmation that what you believe is the correct site of the labs really is just that. Let me run this plan by Moshe Feingold and see what he thinks."

David and Helga agreed that this seemed to be the best approach and left the building.

That evening in the communal dinner room, Helga came up with a suggestion that really startled David.

Helga had suddenly looked at David over her coffee cup and said, "David, it seems to me that we need to make it easier to work together. There is a two-bedroom apartment available in this building, which also has an office. Maybe you and I should move into that apartment and share it."

For a few seconds, David was so surprised that he really was not sure what to say. Finally, he nodded and agreed. They decided that the next day they would both move into the shared apartment.

May 21, 1957
Jerusalem, Israel
Mossad Headquarters

DAVID AND HELGA, now living in a common apartment but in the same building as before, were still waiting for some kind of response from Manny Epstein. Finally, that day, they received a summons to his office. They went there, and Manny asked them to sit down. Manny then told them that their flight to Cairo had been approved. David was to choose an aircraft from the single-engine and twin-engine small planes that the Mossad kept at the Tel Aviv airport. Manny gave David a list of those aircraft to look over. After looking at the list, David chose a Cessna 310, a low-wing, four-seat twin-engine aircraft that was relatively speedy. The 310 had a cruise speed of around 205 mph, a range of 1,000 nautical miles, and a ceiling of 20,000 feet. David was familiar with the model, having flown it occasionally at Aero Clubs located on U.S. Air Force bases where he had been stationed while in the U.S. Air Force. Manny explained that for missions such as theirs, the aircraft would be carrying a phony tail number. The Tel Aviv Control Tower, as well as the area Air Route Control Center, would know of their true identity. The flight, including the detour by way of the vicinity of southern Lebanon, would be approximately 600 miles long each way, well within the range of the Cessna 310.

Manny also suggested that they carry a telephoto camera, which would enable them to try to get photos from a distance of the suspected labs. Helga considered this an excellent idea, but she was concerned that while they were on the ground at Cairo International Airport, ground personnel might see the camera and become suspicious. Manny agreed this could be a problem. Helga then came up with the idea of a small overnight bag that could hold the actual telephoto camera in pieces, together with some toiletries and clothes. Manny said he would have such a bag furnished by the Mossad laboratory staff. With all of that agreed to, David and Helga left the Mossad Headquarters and returned to their apartment.

May 23, 1957
Jerusalem, Israel
Mossad Residence

DAVID AND HELGA WAITED in their apartment for the word that their mission had been approved. Both were impatient and tense, knowing the coming flight and stopover at the Cairo International Airport could prove to be dangerous. Finally, Helga suggested that she show David some of the tourist attractions in Jerusalem and the nearby areas. David agreed, and Helga spent that day driving them around Jerusalem.

Helga was still very quiet, and David was careful to not try to force extra conversation. However, he had a gut feeling that Helga was beginning to come out of her self-imposed shell and, further, was looking at David not just as another agent but as an individual to be respected.

May 24, 1957
Tel Aviv Beach, Israel

WITH STILL NO WORD from the Mossad, and it being a hot and muggy day, Helga suggested they drive to Tel Aviv and go swimming at one of that city's beaches. David thought that was a great idea, and so off they went. They got to the beach, spread out their beach towels, and removed their outer clothes. David was shocked to discover how truly gorgeous and voluptuous Helga's figure was, which she had kept somewhat hidden with loose clothing. Remembering what he had been told of Helga's past, David reminded himself to put aside any romantic ideas that he might have had about her. David took a quick dip in the sea and then lay down on his towel. Helga had gone into the water and was swimming back and forth. After a while, the warm sun made David drowsy, and he fell into a light sleep while lying on his back. Some time later, he felt someone shaking him. He opened his eyes and saw Helga bending over him.

Helga said, "David, you are beginning to get a sunburn. You'd better turn over."

David smiled, said thank you, and did as Helga suggested. Shortly, he was dozing again.

David and Helga swam some more and then returned to their apartment. It had been a lazy but satisfying day for David. He only wished he could stop thinking about Helga in the way he did. He was pretty sure it would be a dead-end path that could result in a major problem between them.

That evening, in the communal dining room, Helga was even more silent than usual. To David, she seemed distracted. David made no effort to break the silence, and after dinner they went back to their common apartment, said good night, and retired to their individual bedrooms.

May 25, 1957
Jerusalem, Israel
Mossad Headquarters

FINALLY, THE SUMMONS came from the Mossad Headquarters. David and Helga went there and discovered that they were to meet not only with Moshe Feingold and Manny Epstein but also with another individual from the U.S. Embassy, who was not introduced. Feingold welcomed them and, as usual, got right down to business.

Feingold said, "David and Helga, this plan of yours to fly to Cairo by way of Lebanon has been approved. However, it is definitely considered a bit risky. But everyone involved agrees it is really necessary to go ahead with it. We absolutely need to pinpoint the exact location of this snake-pit, that is, the location of the labs."

"Now, we have added a couple of thoughts. If an Egyptian fighter comes snooping around, that telephoto camera you'll be carrying would probably be a dead giveaway. So, if a fighter intercepts your flight, then, Helga, you have to slip the camera under your seat very quickly. We have also scrapped the idea of carrying the camera in a small overnight bag if you decide to go into the terminal. We believe that after you land, you should put the camera in the luggage compartment or under the seat. O.K.?"

Helga nodded that she understood.

"David, when you land in Cairo, do not leave the airport. Just go into the terminal, get something to eat or just a drink, then get refueled and fly back here. Your return flight should be at an altitude of 10,000 feet so as to reduce any suspicion on the part of the Egyptians. You'll fly back by way of near Lebanon again in case Egypt is tracking you on their radar. Understood?"

David nodded and said, "Yes sir, all that makes perfect sense. We'll be careful, I can promise you that!"

A few additional items were discussed, then the meeting adjourned, and David and Helga returned to their apartment. Dinner that evening was even quieter than usual. David was thinking about the upcoming flight and did not notice that Helga was even more silent than usual, immersed in her own thoughts.

5

May 26, 1957
Tel Aviv, Israel
Ben Gurion International Airport

THE DAY DAWNED SUNNY AND CLEAR, IDEAL WEATHER FOR the mission.

David and Helga woke up early and headed out to the airport. There, they went directly to the Cessna airplane that the Mossad assigned to them. David, always a careful pilot, preflighted the airplane thoroughly. He walked around the Cessna 310 checking the landing gear and wheel tires, the flaps, and the tail surfaces. Then he climbed on the wings and checked that the two fuel tanks were filled to the top. Finally, he opened the engine cowlings on the two engines and made sure the oil sticks showed full oil levels.

Satisfied that the aircraft was ready for flight, he and Helga climbed aboard. David checked that Helga was strapped in securely, was comfortable, and able to hear on the headphones they both wore.

Using the proper checklist, David fired up the two Continental engines and then contacted the Control Tower for permission to taxi. David used the phony call sign provided by the Mossad, which was "Bluebird 11."

David radioed, “Ground, Bluebird 11 ready to taxi from general aviation parking.”

Ben Gurion Tower radioed back, “Bluebird 11, clear to taxi to Runway 36, hold short behind the TWA Constellation. Wind is northeast variable at 10 to 15.”

David acknowledged the instructions, then taxied slowly to the proper position behind the big TWA transport. There, he completed his engine run-ups.

That done, David turned to Helga, who seemed rather nervous.

He looked at her and, with a smile, said, “Don’t be nervous, Helga. This is going to be a piece of cake!”

Helga did not reply, merely looked at David and nodded.

The TWA flight taxied onto the runway and, with a roar, rolled down the runway and took off. David waited patiently for his take-off clearance. Finally, it came through.

“Bluebird 11, cleared to Runway 36, cleared to Beirut, Lebanon at 3,000 feet VFR. Hold for take-off clearance.”

Now moving more quickly, David slowly taxied to the head of the designated runway and waited for his take-off clearance.

David turned to Helga, gave her a reassuring wink, and asked, “All set, Helga?”

Helga said nothing, merely looked at him, and nodded.

The Control Tower radioed, “Bluebird 11, clear for immediate take-off, clear to climb to and maintain 3,000 feet, clear to a northerly heading.”

David acknowledged the clearance, smoothly advanced the two throttles to take-off power, and as they began their take-off, radioed the Tower, “Bluebird 11 rolling.”

Immediately after take-off, David retracted the landing gear. He leveled off at a mere 1,000 feet of altitude and headed slightly northeast over the blue sea. Then he retracted the flaps. David had already been advised the day before that the Control Tower expected him to fly a different pattern than what his flight plan called for.

They flew northeast toward Lebanon for a few minutes until they were close to the Lebanese border. Then David turned the airplane southwest. Over the Mediterranean Sea, he climbed to 7,500 feet and set up a heading direct to Cairo. Now able to relax, he turned to see how Helga was doing.

David asked, "Helga, is everything O.K.?"

Helga nodded to indicate she was fine and then said, "David, you seem very comfortable flying an airplane."

David responded, "I am. Keep in mind, I flew as a pilot for the U.S. Air Force for a number of years. Furthermore, I was in command of C-130 Hercules attack transports, which are far more complex than this Cessna."

Helga said, "Oh, yes, I had forgotten that."

Then she became very quiet again. They flew on under a brilliant sun over the water and in smooth air. As they approached the coast of Egypt, Helga took the special camera out of its case and set it up to take photos.

Nearing the coast of Egypt, David suddenly received a radio message that used the Cessna's false tail number.

"Cessna 1328 Tango, this is Cairo Air Route traffic Control Center. Do you read?"

David answered without delay.

"Cairo Center, this is Cessna 1328 Tango. Go ahead."

"CEESNA 1328 Tango, radar has been tracking you, but we did not see you departing from Beirut. How come, over?"

"Cairo Center, Cessna 1328 Tango. We were told to stay low because of other traffic, over."

Cairo Center remained silent for some seconds, but finally acknowledged.

David said to Helga, "Somebody was sure paying attention to us. Good thing we were very careful!"

Helga quietly agreed.

They crossed the Egyptian coast, and David began a normal descent into Cairo Airport following the instructions radioed by the Cairo Airport Control Tower.

During the descent, Helga began searching for any sign of a construction site, which they suspected was located near the area where they had been stopped by guards when they had been in Cairo a few days earlier. David turned the aircraft slightly and told Helga to be ready to use the camera. He positioned the aircraft so that the construction site, if it was there, might be on the right side, thus making it easier for Helga to take photos.

As they got closer to the suspected area, Helga began taking photos, and within a very short time, they were past, and Helga put the camera back into its case and hid it under her seat. Luckily, no Egyptian fighter had come up to challenge them. David, following the instructions from the Cairo Airport Control Tower very carefully, made his approach to the airport. He reduced power, lowered the flaps to ten degrees, and then used the fake registration number painted on the aircraft as a call sign. As they approached the airport, he lowered the flaps some more, put the propellers in high pitch, increased power, finally lowered the flaps all the way, and extended the landing gear. David lined up the Cessna with the assigned runway and touched smoothly. In short order, they taxied to the general aviation part of the airfield.

David parked the Cessna, shut down the engines, and he and Helga got out. She was careful to place the camera in the luggage compartment, which David then locked securely. After asking the ground attendant to refuel the aircraft and check the oil levels in both engines, the couple hitched a ride to the terminal to get a bite to eat.

As they entered the restaurant, Helga suddenly turned toward David and buried her head against his shoulder at the same time, grabbing one of his arms in an iron grip. David looked down and realized Helga had turned white as a sheet. David asked, “Helga, are you feeling sick?”

Helga turned her head toward David and whispered, “David, see that big man over there with the beard and the bull neck? I would recognize him anywhere! That’s Rochman, the ‘Butcher of Treblinka!’”

Just then, the head waiter approached them, and David asked for a table near a big plate-glass window, which was far away from where Rochman and others were sitting. He ordered a glass of wine for Helga, hoping that the wine would calm her down. After they ordered some lunch, Helga leaned over and, in a low voice, explained her reaction to David.

“David, I’m sure that man is Rochman. I was a prisoner at Treblinka, and I saw him send my parents to the gas chamber. Not long afterwards, he raped me, more than once. I’m telling you, the man is vicious and evil and a fanatic. If he is here in Cairo, then I feel sure the other two Nazi Colonels must be here too. Remember, we were briefed that three Nazi Colonels were supposed to be in Egypt working on some crazy plan! Rochman was mentioned as one of the three Colonels. Still, it was a shock to actually see him! I’m sorry I had such a violent reaction, but maybe you can understand why!”

David leaned over and gently took Helga’s hand. She did not draw away.

Speaking in a low voice, David said, “Helga, I’m truly sorry this happened to you today. It’s not surprising that you reacted as you did. But now you can see how our mission may be vital not only for Israel but maybe even to the whole Middle East!”

Helga nodded her agreement and then lapsed into her customary silence.

The two agents ate their lunch quickly, and when finished,

managed to leave the restaurant without Rochman noticing them.

Then they returned to their aircraft. Helga took the telephoto camera out of the luggage compartment, and the two of them climbed aboard the Cessna. David fired up the two engines. The Control Tower asked David his destination, and he simply responded that they were returning to Beirut, Lebanon, flying VFR at an altitude of 8,500 feet. After some hesitation, the Tower finally cleared them for take-off, and David wasted no time getting airborne.

As they climbed away from Cairo, Helga prepared to take more photos of the suspected construction site.

They approached the suspected site and Helga began taking photos, while David looked around to try and spot any fighter aircraft that might be intercepting them, but none appeared. Once they reached the Mediterranean Sea, David drew a deep breath of relief and relaxed, enjoying the feeling of flying. Once or twice, he turned his head and looked at Helga, but she appeared to be immersed deep in her thoughts once again, and he thought it better to not intrude.

With the Cessna 310 cruising at over 200 miles an hour, it was not long before they were approaching the northern coast of Israel, just south of the Lebanese border. David put the Cessna in a rapid descent and just before crossing into Lebanon turned back south. He contacted the Ben Gurion Airport Control Tower, and shortly thereafter, they landed there.

Leaving the airport, the agents drove directly to the Mossad Headquarters in order to have their camera film processed.

With that done, the two agents returned to their apartment. Helga was more silent than ever. While they relaxed in the living room watching a TV news program, David caught Helga watching him from time to time. He really didn't know what to make of that and decided to pretend that he hadn't noticed her glances. They had dinner in the communal dining hall with another couple and then both retired early.

May 27, 1957.
Jerusalem, Israel
Mossad Headquarters

DAVID AND HELGA WENT to breakfast, and when they returned to their apartment, there was a phone call from the Mossad Headquarters asking that they appear at 10 a.m. When they arrived, they were directed to the usual conference room where Manny Epstein awaited them. He greeted them and then pointed to a collection of photo enlargements lying on the table. Epstein said, "Take a look at the photos Helga shot. I think you may find them quite interesting."

David and Helga examined the photos silently. When done, David looked up at Epstein and said, "That one area where there is construction looks interesting. But what is it that's being built there? I can't tell."

Epstein replied, "Exactly! Neither can any of our experts. But we believe this may be the site of whatever is being cooked up by those Nazis. Incidentally, Helga, I heard that you recognized Colonel Rochman at the Cairo Airport. I am truly sorry you had to go through that, but it was a very important piece of information since it more or less confirmed the presence of those three Nazis."

"We have arranged for you two to take a trip on one of the Israeli Navy motor torpedo boats. The MTB will drop you off at night on a deserted stretch of Egyptian beach that is a few miles from the construction site. From that spot, you should be able to hike to the village that you visited when you were in Cairo back in the middle of May and drove around. That grocery store in the village appears to be supplying the construction site with food supplies. Based on your conversation with the owner of the store, Abdul, it's possible that he's sympathetic toward Israel. Part of your assignment is to contact that man again and see if he can help us get information on the construction site."

"But there is more. The Mossad was contacted by a technician who will be working in the lab set up by the Nazis. He is Egyptian but hates Nasser and hates the Nazis even more. He is frightened by what he has learned the Nazis are planning. His first name is Alex. He managed to contact us once directly, but feels he cannot do that again because it is too dangerous for himself and his family. Part of your mission is to assist Abdul in figuring out how to contact Alex. This is critical since Alex appears to be our only direct source of information that is actually working inside what we call the labs."

"When you are done, you'll contact the same motor torpedo boat with a small radio we'll give you and arrange for a pick up. That's the mission!"

David couldn't help saying sarcastically, "I'm sure glad it's that simple! A piece of cake!"

Epstein laughed, and even Helga smiled.

Epstein continued his briefing. "There are a number of things you need to know in order to complete this mission. The MTB is one that was specially modified for the Mossad. It is somewhat faster than the sister MTBs in the Israeli Navy. It also has the ability to muffle its engine noise when traveling at slow speeds. The skipper of the MTB will drop you off about a mile or less off the shore near a spot where he has been before. An inflatable craft will take you to the beach and return to the MTB. The skipper has orders to loiter a certain distance offshore until he receives your signal to pick you up. Near the spot where you'll be dropped off, there is a dirt road about a mile inland that leads directly to that small village that you visited once before."

Epstein stopped his briefing to drink some coffee, then continued.

"The nights at this time of the year are short, as I'm sure you know. After you reach shore, I would recommend that you hike to that dirt road, follow it for about a mile or two. Then get off the road and find a place to lie down and get some rest until the sun is well above the horizon. At that point, if you follow the dirt road for another few miles, it will lead you to that small village. There, I would recommend that you find a place to have some breakfast. When you are done with that, it should be late enough in the morning to go to the grocery store whose owner is your contact. At around noon, which is siesta time in Egypt, he will take you to his home where you can rest and talk."

Epstein stopped again to drink more coffee and organize his thoughts, and then once again continued his briefing.

"Now, your actual mission will be to talk to this storekeeper. He was contacted some time ago, and we believe that he is an Israeli sympathizer, hates the government of Egypt, and is very concerned as to what that nearby construction is really all about. He has a wife and three small children. His wife feels the same as he does. We at the Mossad feel that we need more information before moving against whatever those Nazi fanatics have in mind. We cannot risk an all-out war."

Epstein paused again, and neither David nor Helga said a word. Then Epstein began talking again.

"Your cover story will be that you are archeologists and that you have heard stories from other archeologists that there may be unknown buried sites thousands of years old in that general area. You will be carrying some typical archeological equipment and will travel with U.S. passports. We'll equip you with compasses, maps, and rations as well as water."

"Finally, it would be greatly appreciated if you got back in one piece and unharmed!"

This time, not only did David laugh, but even Helga had a little giggle. Epstein provided the two agents with some additional detailed instructions. Then they were led to an equipment room and outfitted with clothes, fake passports, and some fairly light equipment to carry on their incursion into Egypt. The two agents loaded Helga's car and returned to their apartment.

Dinner that evening was very quiet as both David and Helga thought about the upcoming mission.

May 28, 1957
Ashdod, Israel
Israelí Navy Harbor

IN THE EVENING, David and Helga reported aboard the motor torpedo boat (MTB) assigned to their mission. This was an eighty-foot-long boat whose design was based on the World War II American torpedo boats. They met its captain, Eric Levy, an American who had served on MTBs in the U.S. Navy in World War II before emigrating to Israel. Levy was a tall man with a beard that made him look like a pirate and a twinkle in his eyes. He welcomed them aboard and showed them where they could relax and rest in the small wardroom below deck. The crew cast off as soon as they were aboard, and the MTB moved slowly and quietly out of the harbor. The night was moonless and thus very dark, precisely what was needed for this mission. Once a mile out, the captain increased speed to 25 knots, and the MTB headed for the specific spot on the Egyptian coast that was their destination.

May 29, 1957
North of Cairo, Egypt
Village Near Labs

SOMETIME LATER, approaching the coast of Egypt, but still about four miles out, Captain Levy slowed the MTB to a crawl and engaged the engine mufflers. When about a mile from shore,

Captain Levy shut down the engines and let the MTB just drift. An inflatable craft was made ready and was lowered over the side.

Captain Levy took the two agents aside and said to them, "I hope you two have been briefed on the patrols that walk along the shore. They always have dogs with them. So watch your step. Once you get about a mile inland, you should be safe from such patrols. But be very careful at all times!"

Helga said, "Thank you for your concern, Captain. Believe me, we plan on being extremely careful!"

Captain Levy shook hands with the two agents, wished them a safe journey, and told them the MTB would be waiting a few miles offshore for their return. David, Helga, and two crewmen were hustled aboard the inflatable. The two crewmen paddled silently toward the invisible beach. There was a small amount of surf that presented no problem, and then the inflatable ran aground on the beach. David and Helga jumped off the inflatable. One of the two crewmen shook their hands, whispered "good luck," and the inflatable disappeared into the dark night on its way back to the MTB.

David and Helga immediately began walking silently inland, looking for the dirt road that had been mentioned in their briefing. Neither said a word as they dimly managed to find the dirt road. After an hour of following the dirt road, David suggested they stop until sunrise. They turned off the dirt road and, walking very slowly and carefully, managed to find what they believed to be a small hill. They climbed over the top of the hill and sat down in the sand on the other side. They used the rucksacks they had been carrying as pillows and lay down beside each other. David hesitantly reached over and found Helga's hand, which she did not withdraw. Thus lying beside each other, they tried to get some sleep.

A few hours later, David woke up with the sun shining in his eyes. He sat upright and discovered that Helga was no longer beside him. Looking around, he spotted her lying just below the crest of the hill behind which they had slept. She was obviously checking to see if there was any traffic on the dirt road. She turned around and came to sit beside him.

Helga said, "Good Morning, David. Hope you slept well."

David said he had. Then Helga asked," Should we begin walking toward the village where we make contact?"

David looked at his watch and saw that it was already close to 9 a.m. He agreed that it was time to get moving. Shouldering their rucksacks, they set off along the dirt road, hoping that they would not meet anyone.

The two agents walked along the dirt road, not saying anything, each absorbed in their own thoughts. As the sun rose higher, the day got hotter. An hour and a half later, they saw their destination in the distance.

They approached the village carefully and discovered it was considerably larger than they had realized during their previous visit. Walking down what appeared to be the main street of the village, they eventually found a small cafe that was open. They went inside, and Helga, who spoke fluent Arabic, ordered some breakfast. The cafe was empty, and the employees paid them no particular attention.

They ate their breakfast silently, not wanting to attract any more attention than was necessary. After finishing their meal, David paid with Egyptian currency that they had been issued by the Mossad. Then the two wandered slowly around the village. They eventually found the grocery store where they were to make contact with the owner.

The store had not opened yet, so David and Helga wandered around the village looking at the various shops. To David's surprise, it turned out that Helga had an eye for curios and small artistic items. When he asked her about it, she replied that she had been taking art classes when not out on assignment.

Around 10:30, the grocery store finally opened, but when David and Helga came by, it was busy with a considerable number of shoppers. So the two wandered around some more before finally returning to the store. This time, they were the only shoppers. Abdul spotted them and, remembering who they were, his face broke out in a broad smile. He addressed them in good English and told them he was going to close the store for the noonday siesta in a few minutes. Shortly thereafter, he closed the store and led them to his house, which was on the edge of town. There they met the owner's wife, a young and pretty woman who also spoke English, and their three very young children. Abdul's wife quickly prepared a simple meal for the agents and for her family. After the meal was finished, Abdul suggested the two agents follow him to a small living room where he could pass on whatever information he had.

Abdul began by informing them that his store was supplying the groceries for the construction crews working on the labs. He was also selling food to a servant from a house not far from the construction site, where he had learned the Nazis and their concubines resided.

Abdul did not know much about the labs under construction, except that they were being built underground below what was supposed to be a textile mill. The below-ground part of the building appeared to have some laboratories as well as areas for manufacturing something, he knew not what. Abdul believed the site was still at least two to three months from being completed.

The two agents found all of this info very interesting, but not complete enough to give a whole picture as to what was going to take place at the site. David also asked Abdul to keep his eyes open for a technician named Alex, whom the agents hoped to eventually meet. It was made clear to Abdul that if he was able to get more information or was able to contact the technician called Alex, the two agents could return on short notice.

At the end of the briefing, David gave Abdul a packet of Egyptian currency that Epstein had given him to carry and give to Abdul with the caution that he should spend it carefully and not flash it around in order to prevent anyone from becoming suspicious. Abdul was very grateful and recommended that the two agents lie down in the small bedroom and try to get some sleep. He said his wife was going to feed them some dinner that evening, and then when darkness came, he would take them to the dirt road and then would lead them back to the coast and the pick-up point where they would meet the same MTB in the middle of the night.

The two agents rested until dinner time. When total darkness came, Abdul led them to the dirt road and then to a point on the beach close to where they had originally landed. He wished them good luck and disappeared into the night. David and Helga sat down on the beach, and David used the low-power transmitter to contact the MTB waiting a few miles offshore. The MTB had spent the previous day loitering some thirty miles north of the Egyptian coast. Now, receiving the signal, the captain turned south and headed for the same spot where the two agents had been put ashore.

While David and Helga waited patiently for the return of the MTB, they discussed their visit with Abdul in low voices.

David said, "We didn't accomplish much on this trip. But I thought Abdul was sincere and could be trusted."

Helga agreed and said, "I talked with his wife for a while. She actually attended the University of Cairo for two years, one of the very few women who were able to go to the university. It was there that she met Abdul."

David said, "Interesting. I had the feeling that both Abdul

and his wife were educated. They certainly seem to hate the government that has Nasser as a dictator. And Abdul made it clear that he really fears the three Nazis and whatever they are up to."

Helga agreed and said, "His wife is equally frightened by whatever is going on near them. But David, we are not bringing back much information to Epstein. He will be disappointed."

David wasn't so sure. He said, "Look, Helga, Epstein is a realist and he's been in the intelligence game a long time. I don't think he expected great results from this trip. Let's wait and see what he says."

Helga agreed, and the two agents became silent as they awaited the return of the MTB, all the while keeping a sharp lookout for any coast patrols.

Eventually, they heard some muffled noises, and then a low voice came out of the darkness and asked if they were there. The two quickly walked down to the water's edge, boarded the inflatable, and were paddled back to the MTB, where Captain Levy greeted them. Once underway, the agents stretched out below deck and rested until they finally reached Ashdod harbor in Israel. Then they drove back to the Mossad residence and slept for a few hours.

May 31, 1957
Jerusalem, Israel
Mossad Headquarters

In the afternoon, Epstein summoned David and Helga to his office. There, they passed on what little information they had gathered. David commented that the entire trip seemed to have been a waste of time and resources, but Epstein disagreed.

Epstein said, "Look, David, it takes time to develop a complete picture of what is going on over there. In the meantime, we now have a direct link to the labs via Abdul and through him to this technician, Alex. That alone is extremely valuable."

Once more, David disagreed. He said, "But Manny, Israel should be planning a military strike against those labs. I get the feeling nothing is happening!"

Epstein patiently explained the situation to David.

Epstein said, "David, if Israel destroyed those labs right now, it could well be a political disaster. The entire world would want to know what in heaven's name we were doing, destroying a half-built textile mill. We need a lot more evidence as to what those Nazi scientists are planning to do. Furthermore, if we strike too soon, Nasser will simply build another set of labs somewhere else. So you see, first of all, the site must be completed, and the real work there must begin. Then, and only then, can Israel mount an attack that will not only destroy those labs but also the people directing the whole operation."

Epstein stopped, then continued.

"David, do you see now why we need more information and also why we must be patient?"

David grudgingly agreed and waited to hear what the next step would be.

Epstein continued his explanation of what needed to be done next.

He said, "I think the connection we now have with Abdul and through him with Alex could turn out to be vital. But in the meantime, do you see why we need to be patient and wait for the construction of those labs to be completed? For now, David and Helga, you can have a well-deserved vacation. So go on back to your apartment and just wait for me to contact you."

David and Helga both nodded and drove back to their apartment. That evening, David suggested that they go to the beach the following day. Helga thought that was a fine idea.

June 1, 1957
Tel Aviv, Israel
Mediterranean Sea Beach

DAVID AND HELGA lay on the beach enjoying the warmth of the sun. The beach was quiet with not many people there. Eventually, David said he was going for a dip and asked Helga if she would like to join him. She agreed, and the two walked into the water, got through the surf, and swam for a bit. At one point, Helga got very close to David, and her very full breast brushed briefly against him. David involuntarily stiffened at the unexpected contact. As both treaded water, Helga gave David a long look. He was unsure how to react. David had already realized that Helga attracted him greatly, but based on what little he knew of her past history, he hesitated to show his true feelings. He realized she was scarred emotionally from her experiences at the Treblinka Execution Camp and at the hands of the brutal Colonel Rochman.

After their swim, they lay down on their beach towels and soon David fell into a shallow sleep. He woke to find that a young man unknown to him was talking to Helga and obviously trying to start a relationship. Helga made it very clear to the stranger that she was not interested in his rather clumsy advances, but he continued undeterred. David said nothing for a while, then decided he had heard enough. He stood up, approached the young man, and in a quiet yet forceful tone of voice said, "Mister, the lady is simply not interested in what you are selling. I strongly recommend you leave her alone!"

The stranger looked at David, laughed, and in an insulting and arrogant tone of voice snarled, "Take a hike, fella!"

That was a bit too much for David. Moving very quickly, he got close to the young man, grabbed him in an Oriental defense grip he had been taught in the U.S. Air Force, and tossed him down onto the sand.

Helga, who had been watching David's reaction, just stood there and laughed. The young man struggled to his feet and slunk off.

Helga came close to David and said softly, "Thank you, David. I was trying to avoid a noisy argument with that guy. Otherwise, I might have done something similar to what you did!"

David said, "Good thing I beat you to it. You'd probably have broken his neck!"

Helga laughed at that while David merely smiled and lay down again.

Driving back to their apartment, Helga was considerably more talkative than usual. She wondered what was in store for the two of them during the remainder of their mission.

Helga said, "David, it seems to me that we didn't get much information on that last trip to Egypt".

David agreed. "No, we sure didn't. But Helga, maybe it is simply too soon to get much info. It's possible that we all have to wait until all the construction is completed and the actual work of the labs begins. Manny certainly seems to think so."

Helga said, "I think you are absolutely correct. I guess I am just very anxious to kill that entire project."

David said, "Of course you are. And you should be. There is no telling what those Nazi fanatics are going to cook up. But Helga, keep in mind that once the labs are completed, it will take months for them to create whatever weapons they have in mind. I think Manny is absolutely right when he says that the labs need to be destroyed at the right time and not a moment too soon. I've really changed my mind as to the timing of the destruction of the site."

Helga agreed and then fell silent.

When they reached their apartment, David went in first and

turned on the light in the living room. As he turned around, there suddenly was Helga with her arms around him, holding him tightly.

She kissed David passionately, and he responded. Then he felt her tongue entering his mouth, and his organ responded automatically. After a few minutes, Helga loosened her grip slightly, stopped kissing him, and looked up at him.

Helga said in a soft voice, "Are you upset I did that, David?"

David responded, "Upset? I'm delighted! I think I fell in love with you quite a while ago, but didn't know how to tell you!"

Helga said, "I'm so glad to hear that! I want you to make love to me! But please be gentle. No man has made love to me since I came out of Treblinka!"

David said, "I think I understand Helga. Shall we go to bed?"

Without any hesitation, Helga said yes, and they both peeled off their bathing suits.

David suspected that after the horrors of Treblinka, Helga had involuntarily erected both physical and emotional barriers. Now, sensing that David was both gentle and understanding, Helga's barriers had begun to crumble, and as a young and healthy woman, she reacted very positively to David. After years of suppressing her sexual needs, they now came alive very passionately.

Lying in bed close together, they began kissing again. David stroked her full breasts and then took her nipples in his mouth one at a time. At the same time, he gently stroked her clitoris, and she stroked his penis. Their breathing quickened more and more, and Helga began moaning. Finally, David felt Helga shuddering as she had an orgasm. They lay there quietly for a short time, and then Helga said very softly, "Please, David, come inside me!"

He very slowly and gently entered her, and she gasped. David wasn't sure if she was having a bad reaction because of the rape she had suffered years before. But then she began moving up and down, French kissing him at the same time, and it wasn't long before they had simultaneous orgasms. Afterwards, they lay together without saying anything.

David fell asleep for a short time. He woke up to feel Helga moving up and down beside him. He responded, and they made love again. Then both fell into a deep sleep for a number of hours.

6

June 2-5, 1957
Jerusalem, Israel
Mossad Residence

THE NEXT FEW DAYS PASSED WITH NO CALLS FROM ANYONE at the Mossad. David and Helga reveled in their newfound love. For David, the feelings he felt for Helga were something new and different, unlike anything he had experienced in past relationships. When they went down to the communal dining room, other Mossad agents took note of what appeared to be a totally different relationship between the two agents. In the meantime, David and Helga wondered what would be in store for them in the near future.

Because they had time on their hands, they both took pleasure in exploring Jerusalem as well as other parts of Israel. Helga was very familiar with Jerusalem, having lived there for a number of years. She took genuine pleasure in showing David around, and he, in turn, could hardly believe the transformation that had overtaken Helga. She smiled a lot, sometimes laughed, and talked to David a great deal more. He, in turn, someone who was often silent, also began to talk more and to reveal his feelings to Helga.

And so the two agents spent a few wonderful days getting to finally know each other much better.

June 6, 1957
Jerusalem, Israel
Mossad Headquarters

THE SUMMONS FROM Mossad finally came one afternoon, and the next morning, the two agents reported to Mossad Headquarters, where both Epstein and Feingold waited for them. When they entered the conference room hand in hand, Epstein had trouble hiding a smile. He had already been alerted to the change in their relationship by a Mossad employee who resided in the same communal building as David and Helga.

Feingold and Epstein welcomed them warmly and offered them cups of coffee. Then Feingold began the meeting.

Feingold said, "You two did a fine job on your last trip into Egypt. Unfortunately, as you already know, we all have to wait for the construction to be finished and the real work of the labs to begin. In the meantime, we feel there is something very important that you can do. Both Manny and I feel that it is critical to establish a more direct link with the technician we call Alex. I'm afraid that means another trip by MTB to Egypt. This time, you will have to stay longer because we don't know how long it will take for Abdul to contact Alex and for Alex to meet with you two."

"I really don't like sending you two in harm's way again so soon, but we believe it is critical at this juncture. David and Helga, how do you feel about going back into Egypt?"

David looked at Helga, who simply smiled at him. Taking this as a sign that he should speak for both of them, he plunged ahead.

David said, "Gentlemen, I think I can speak for both of us.

I agree that while we wait for the labs to be finished, it gives us a span of time during which we should cement good relations with Alex. He may turn out to be the only contact we'll ever have inside the labs."

Moshe Feingold said, "I think David is quite right. Alex could turn out to be a critical source of information. We'll have to really try and get much closer to him. For now, the only way seems to be through Abdul. David and Helga, the Mossad will work on contacting Abdul again. In the meantime, I guess you two get a few more days off."

David and Helga looked at each other and smiled.

Feigned excused himself and left the meeting.

Epstein said, "By the way, my wife Esther wanted me to pass on to you two an invitation to dinner at our house tomorrow evening. Are you available?"

David said, "I think Helga and I are available unless President Nasser of Egypt wants us to have dinner with him!"

Epstein looked startled, then burst out laughing.

He said, "Great! If Nasser calls, tell him you have a prior commitment. Oh, by the way, Esther said she would like for you two to show up around 7:30."

David and Helga both nodded, and the meeting ended.

June 7, 1957
Jerusalem, Israel
The Epstein Residence

As requested, David and Helga showed up right on time at 7:30 at the Epstein residence. David was carrying a bouquet of flowers and Helga a box of Swiss chocolates.

Manny Epstein welcomed them warmly and introduced them to his wife, Esther. She was a tall, slender woman with a beautiful face and hair turning gray. She also welcomed them warmly and thanked them for the flowers and chocolates.

The four sat down for before-dinner drinks.

Manny said, "Esther is a teacher now, but for a while she worked for the Mossad as an analyst. I stole her away from the Mossad and tricked her into marrying me."

With a twinkle in her eyes, Esther said, "Manny still does not know that I stole him."

Everyone had a good laugh over that.

David and Helga felt very comfortable in the company of Manny and Esther. She asked David some questions about his past before he joined the CIA. Helga was quite surprised to learn about some of the events in David's past.

Then Esther said, "There is a rumor going around that you two are becoming a romantic couple. Is there any truth to that?"

Helga looked at David and then very quietly said, "It does feel that way."

Esther positively glowed as she said, "I think you two will be good for each other."

Manny said nothing, just smiled.

After a delicious dinner cooked by Esther, the foursome sat in the living room and discussed various things. Finally, David said that he and Helga should leave since the following day was a regular workday for both Manny and Esther.

As they were saying good night, Esther said, "I hope we'll be seeing more of you. You are a great couple."

Then, she impulsively kissed both David and Helga on the cheeks.

On the way home, Helga said, "They are truly a great couple, I hope we'll see them again!"

David heartily agreed.

June 8-11, 1957
Jerusalem, Israel
Mossad Residence

No one from the Mossad contacted David and Helga for three days. The couple spent the time getting to know each other much better and enjoying their newfound relationship. They talked about their past and went to the beach to lie in the sun and swim. For those few days, they both managed to more or less forget about the events taking place in Egypt and instead reveled in their newfound love. For David, it was the first relationship that truly meant something to him and that made him want to both love and protect this woman. For Helga, it was at last a release from what had been the nightmare that was born while she was a prisoner at the Treblinka Execution Camp.

Finally, on the fourth day, a summons came from Manny Epstein to attend a meeting at the Mossad Headquarters early the following morning.

David said to Helga, "Guess our vacation is over. Oh, well, it was awfully nice while it lasted."

Helga giggled at his remark, something she never would have done a few weeks earlier.

June 12, 1957
Jerusalem, Israel
Mossad Headquarters

David and Helga arrived at the Mossad Headquarters a few minutes early and went directly to the by now familiar conference room. A few minutes later, Epstein entered, followed by Feingold and a third man who was not introduced except that Feingold mentioned that the man represented the Prime

Minister himself. This pronouncement told David and Helga that this meeting was somehow more than routine.

Feingold opened the meeting by welcoming them and thanking them for coming.

Then he said, "It seems that this entire activity in Egypt has attracted the attention of the United States Department of State as well as their military. They asked us if it would be possible for the two of you to visit Washington and make an in-person report. It appears that the U.S. Government is genuinely concerned about this Egyptian operation and what it could mean for the entire Middle East region. The request came directly to the Prime Minister, who approved the trip. I will accompany the two of you on this trip. The idea is for you to brief both the State Dept. and the military."

"In addition, you are to meet two scientists. One is a nuclear scientist who works at the Los Alamos National Laboratory in Los Alamos, New Mexico. The other is an Englishman expert in poison gases who works at the Livermore National Laboratory in Livermore, California."

"For this reason, it was decided that we would first fly to Chicago, where you would meet these scientists, and then afterwards we'd fly to Washington. We leave tomorrow at 11 a.m. on TWA."

Manny Epstein picked up the briefing. He said, "I suggest that the two of you go to Helga's office and try to put together an outline that relates what little we know of this Egyptian operation so far. You might also want to include any ideas you have as to what Egypt is planning. Don't hesitate to bring up whatever you really believe based on what you have seen so far and what you know about the three Nazis running the operation. Helga, you in particular might be in a good position to share your views. Anyhow, that is what the trip is all about."

David and Helga looked at each other and then Helga simply

said, "David and I will spend the rest of the day working on this briefing. We'll do the best we can."

Epstein said approvingly, "I'm sure you will! Have a successful trip!"

With that, the meeting ended. David and Helga immediately retired to her office to work on the briefing document they would use when in both Chicago and Washington. They realized that the trip was important and the briefing even more so.

June 13, 1957
Tel Aviv, Israel
Ben Gurion Airport

David and Helga met Moshe Feingold at the terminal, and shortly they boarded the TWA Jetstream Constellation. The flight operated nonstop to Paris and then nonstop to Chicago. All three agents were traveling First Class. They were served lunch en route to Paris, a five-hour flight. After an hour on the ground, where the three agents wandered around the terminal, they took off on the twelve-hour leg to Chicago.

Over the Atlantic Ocean, TWA served a nice dinner to the First Class passengers. Once that was cleared away, David asked the stewardess if he could visit the flight deck and showed her his CIA identification. She went to ask the Captain and returned shortly to tell David that he was welcome to go there. Helga was half asleep, curled up in her seat. David told her where he was going and then went forward to the flight deck.

The captain welcomed David and introduced him to the First Officer and the Flight Engineer. When David mentioned casually that at one time he had been in the U.S. Air Force and had flown C-130 Hercules attack transports, the conversation became more lively. The First Officer had also flown C-130 aircraft at one time.

David remained on the flight deck for an hour before returning to his seat. He noticed that Feingold was asleep, and so was Helga. He sat down, pulled a blanket over himself, and also fell asleep.

Hours later, the Constellation made landfall over Gander, Newfoundland, Canada, and then flew across Canada and on to Chicago.

At Chicago's Midway Airport, they were met by a government car and driver who took them to downtown Chicago and the Palmer House Hotel, where they spent the night.

June 14, 1957
Chicago, Illinois, USA
Museum of Science and Industry, West Wing

THE NEXT MORNING, after an excellent breakfast, the three agents were driven south along the shore of Lake Michigan to the Museum of Science and Industry. David wondered why they were being taken to a museum of all places, but said nothing. Once there, they were escorted to the west wing of the Museum and to what appeared to be a special entrance that had armed sentries. Then they were brought to a third-floor conference room.

Upon entering the room, David was delighted to see that his handler, Jack Riley, and Ernest Hilliard, the CIA Director of Middle East Operations, were both there. Also in attendance were: Dean Morrison, the CIA Deputy Director of Operations, as well as two distinguished-looking older men.

Dean Morrison chaired the meeting, and after the introductions were finished, began speaking.

"I want to welcome you, David, and I particularly want to welcome you, Miss Horowitz. Your exploits on behalf of the

State of Israel have previously come to the attention of the CIA. It is truly a pleasure to finally meet you."

At that, Helga blushed, and David smiled reassuringly at her.

Morrison continued, "David and Miss Horowitz, I'm pretty sure that you are wondering why this meeting is in a museum. Actually, this is the west wing of the museum and is totally walled off from the rest of the museum itself. It has been used by government agencies since the beginning of World War II."

David nodded his understanding of the somewhat unorthodox location for a top-level secret meeting of government officials.

Morrison continued, "There are two scientists here that I want you to meet. I feel that what they have to say is very important to the conduct of your mission."

With that, Morrison turned to the two distinguished-looking older men. He pointed to a tall, thin man and said, "This is Dr. Daniel Fleishman, who is a leading chemist at the Livermore National Laboratory in Livermore, California."

Morrison then pointed to the other older man, an individual of medium height with a ruddy complexion.

Morrison said, "And this is Dr. Edward Rawling, from the United Kingdom, who is a physicist currently at the Los Alamos National Laboratory in Los Alamos, New Mexico. These two gentlemen have some truly important information they want to share with you two."

Dr. Fleishman picked up the dialogue. He said, "Dr. Rawling and I have heard of your mission, and we know something about those Nazi scientists. You see, at the end of World War II, both of us became part of a task force that was created to find out what the Nazi scientists had been working on. The two that are now in Egypt were of particular interest. As a nuclear scientist, I was interested in Dr. Schweitz, also a nuclear scientist. Dr. Rawling was interested in the work of Dr. Reicher, a chemist who worked on poison gases. Dr. Rawling, why don't you talk about the work of Dr. Reicher?"

Rawling, speaking in a distinctive British accent, began his part of the briefing. He said, "Dr. Reicher was not just working on various kinds of poison gases. It seems that he had managed to successfully perfect a poison gas that was more than merely deadly. This gas, known as Rilin gas, had a special property. After being released into the atmosphere, it would travel a certain distance and then settle on whatever was below. When it settled, it would stick like glue to anything it contacted. It could not be removed or washed off, and it quickly killed any living thing it touched. It was the deadliest poison gas ever created!"

With that, Rawling stopped talking and turned to Fleichman for him to continue.

Fleichman said, "The other Nazi scientist you are interested in was an equally deadly fellow. He developed a tactical nuclear weapon that could be easily dropped from an aircraft or fired from a special cannon, and that was designed to spread radiation over a large area rather than destroying using a big explosion. In other words, it was meant to kill as many people as possible. Dr. Rawling and I have a considerable amount of scientific data regarding the work of these two Nazi scientists, but frankly, I'm not sure it would help you two in your mission. I believe what you heard here today should be sufficient to make it very clear to both of you how dangerous this whole plot is if allowed to be carried out to its completion!"

Flechman hesitated, then finally continued.

He said, "David and Helga, you have to be very clear on how dangerous these two scientists really are. They are not only very intelligent, but they are also psychotic fanatics to whom human life means absolutely nothing. They will stop at nothing to achieve their insane goals. Whatever you do, do not underestimate how potentially dangerous they really are."

After Flechman stopped talking, there was absolute silence as everyone thought about the implications of what they had just heard.

Finally, Morrison continued the narrative.

He said, "Thank you, gentlemen, for your extremely valuable input. Unfortunately, it is also information that is truly frightening. I see this entire Egyptian project as a likely disaster, not just for the State of Israel but potentially also for the entire Middle East. It seems to me that we must destroy the entire project at the appropriate time, but not before. David and Helga, based on what we just heard, I believe your lives will be in extreme danger any time you enter Egypt."

The room was quiet for a minute. Finally, Morrison began speaking again.

He said, "It seems to me that there's little doubt that this whole project must be destroyed, but that to accomplish that, more hard data is an absolute requirement. To me, that means sending David and Helga back into Egypt with the purpose of locating additional sources of information. That will involve a great deal of risk, but I don't see any other way to proceed at this time."

Morrison hesitated a few seconds and then continued.

Morrison said, "I guess that does it for the time being unless anyone else has something more to contribute."

No one said anything.

Hilliard said, "Dr. Fleischman and Dr. Rawling, I think it would be beneficial if you could remain in Chicago an extra day so that if the CIA and the Mossad felt they needed additional information, both of you would be readily available."

Fleischman immediately said, "I certainly agree."

Rawling merely nodded.

Hilliard then said, "David, you might want to spend the rest of the day and part of tomorrow showing Helga some of

Chicago, and then tomorrow evening, fly to Washington. What do you think?"

David looked at Helga, who nodded to show her agreement, and then said, "That's an excellent idea. I think Helga might enjoy getting to know Chicago a bit better."

Helga agreed, and thus the schedule was set. Morrison thanked David and Helga for their participation and told them they were now on their own.

As David and Helga left the conference room, he suggested to Helga that they first take a quick tour of the Museum of Science and Industry. Helga agreed, and they left the West Wing they were in and walked around to the main entrance of the Museum. The two agents toured the very large museum, and Helga proved to be an interested visitor and asked many questions of David, who had previously visited the Museum.

In the afternoon, they toured the downtown area of Chicago known as the Loop, and Helga marveled at the wealth of choices in the many stores.

Then, in the evening, David took Helga to a famous Scandinavian restaurant that featured not only excellent food but a very unique feature. After dinner, the two went to a small theater that was part of the restaurant building. There, a puppet show took place that followed the storyline of a grand opera that played in the background. Helga, who loved classical music, was absolutely delighted and was mesmerized by the entire production. When they finally left the restaurant/theater complex, Helga turned to David and said, "Honey, that was fantastic. Thank you so much for bringing me here!"

David merely smiled and hugged her.

June 15, 1957
Chicago, Illinois, USA
Downtown Area

THE FOLLOWING MORNING, David and Helga visited the three lakefront tourist attractions in Chicago: the Field Museum of Natural History, the Shedd Aquarium, and the Adler Planetarium. Helga appeared to be very interested in all of these tourist sites and was really thrilled to visit the Aquarium and the Planetarium.

At lunchtime, David took them to the nearby Chinatown, where Helga was introduced to Chinese cuisine for the first time.

In the afternoon, they returned to Midway Airport and boarded a flight to Washington. Upon arriving there, they went directly to David's condominium for the night. They knew that the next day they would have to participate in what could prove to be a very important meeting at the famous Pentagon.

June 16, 1957
Washington, DC
The Pentagon

EARLY THE FOLLOWING morning, David and Helga drove to the Pentagon, the huge five-sided building that is the headquarters for all of the U.S. military services. Helga was absolutely overwhelmed by the sheer size of the building, which had been erected in the early 1940s. There, after some delay, they were provided with the proper passes and escorted to a large conference room.

Waiting there were Morrison, Hilliard, and Riley from the CIA and Feingold from the Mossad. In addition, there were other government officials. The U.S. military was represented by two Colonels and one Navy Captain. The U.S. Department of State was also represented by two men.

Morrison began the meeting by welcoming everyone. Then he said, "We are gathered here today because both President Eisenhower and Prime Minister Ben Gurion of Israel are in total agreement that a plot that is being concocted in Egypt by Egyptian President Nasser against the State of Israel is considered to be extremely dangerous. It is directly dangerous for Israel. But it could also indirectly impact the entire Middle East region. Beyond that, it is being looked at as a danger to U.S. interests, plus having the potential to destroy a democracy, namely Israel. We don't know very much about this plot as yet. However, there are two intelligence agents in this room who are directly involved in unraveling this plot. They have been invited here today to brief all of you on what little is known to date. They are Mr. Knox of the CIA and Miss Horowitz of the Israeli Mossad. They are working as a team on this project. Miss Horowitz and Mr. Knox, it's your show."

David and Helga had previously decided on how to organize the briefing. Now David stood up to begin the presentation.

David began, "Gentlemen, the State of Israel received a message from an unknown source about a month ago. It described a meeting organized by President Nasser of Egypt. At the meeting were the President of Syria and the Prime Minister of Jordan., The message said that, in addition, three former top-level Nazi Colonels were present. Two of these are scientists. The message further stated that it was the intent of President Nasser to develop a plot that would result in the total destruction of the State of Israel. The only other info in the message was the code name of this plot against Israel. It was called the 'Sword of Damocles.' That is all the information provided by this unknown source. I will now turn this briefing over to Miss Horowitz of the Mossad."

Before Helga could say anything, Morrison stood up and interrupted.

"Miss Horowitz, please forgive me for interrupting, but I feel there is something I really need to say at this point. Because the CIA and the Mossad are working closely together on this particular project, I have learned quite a bit about Miss Horowitz. She has been one of the Mossad's most successful agents. She is very tenacious and accomplished and has operated against Egypt on a number of missions. She also happens to be multilingual. If she wasn't already an employee of the Mossad, I would steal her for the CIA. Gentlemen, I give you Miss Horowitz!"

With that, Morrison sat down as those present applauded. Helga stood up and began speaking. As she did, Dvid was struck by her commanding presence. She appeared to be totally comfortable addressing the assembled group of high-level military and government officials.

"Good morning, gentlemen, and thank you, Mr. Morrison, for those kind words. Unfortunately, neither Mr. Knox nor I can provide a great deal of information at this point. The secret source that originally alerted the Mossad about this plot indicated that they would no longer be in a position to send any additional information."

"The mere fact that the political heads of three Arab countries that all border Israel met secretly is enough to be considered a reason for alarm. Then there is also the presence of the three Nazi Colonels, all of whom are on the list of World War II war criminals. The two scientists have a record of accomplishments in the area of destructive weapons, which in and of itself should be frightening to all of you. As to the third Colonel, he is a sadistic killer who truly enjoys first torturing and then killing people. This I know from personal experience. But what this all adds up to is still not clear."

Helga stopped for a few seconds. No one said a word. Then she continued.

"Thanks to Mr. Knox, we were able to pinpoint the exact location of a building that is under construction in northern Egypt between Cairo and Alexandria. We believe it is a fake hosiery textile mill at ground level with research and manufacturing areas below ground level. We have also located an Egyptian storekeeper located in a village near this building who appears to be totally opposed to the Nasser regime and the 'Sword of Damocles' project."

Again, Helga stopped for a few seconds, then continued.

"Mr. Knox and I were briefed two days ago by a nuclear scientist and an expert in poison gases. These gentlemen knew a great deal about the work that the Nazi scientists had accomplished during World War II. That information was enough to terrify any sane person. Mr. Morrison was present at that briefing, and I believe he will agree that I am not exaggerating one bit!"

Morrison interrupted to say forcefully, "I totally agree with Miss Horowitz!"

Helga resumed her briefing.

"Mr. Morrison, thank you for your comment. I want to point out that the entire State of Israel actually occupies a very small patch of land. That fact makes the potential danger of the Nazi weapons even more dangerous."

"Mr. Knox and I are in total agreement that, for the immediate future, the best course of action is to try and find someone sympathetic to Israel who is associated in some way with the building that we know is the actual site of this plot. In the meantime, it is likely that we have to wait for the entire building to be completed. While the building is still under construction, it gives us an opportunity to try to penetrate this whole plot by locating someone who is involved in the plot in some way but is opposed to its goals."

"Mr. Knox and I both feel that we shall have to enter Egypt again, possibly a number of times. Based on what we have seen so far, that should be possible with a minimum of danger. Other than that, we really have no other information at this time. However, we are open to any ideas any of you may have."

With that, Helga stopped speaking and waited to see if anyone had any different ways to approach the problem, but the room remained silent.

Finally, Helga asked, "Does anyone have any questions?"

A government official stood up and asked, "Miss Horowitz, is it really that easy for the two of you to enter Egypt?"

Helga answered, "We have two advantages. First, we believe that Nasser himself has no inkling that someone has revealed the existence of his plot to the State of Israel. Second, those Nazi scientists are also likely to consider themselves too smart for anyone to short-circuit their insane plan. That is a common fallacy of the Nazis, as shown in World War II. However, Mr. Knox and I are very aware of the dangers that may be present every time we are inserted into Egypt."

There being no more questions, Morrison stood and thanked both Helga and David for their briefings.

Then he said, "It appears that there is nothing more to discuss until such time as more hard information can be gathered. Thank you all for coming today."

With that, the meeting adjourned. Feingold informed David and Helga that the schedule called for them to stay in Washington the rest of that day. The next day, they were to take the train to New York City and remain there for the day and the following day until the evening, when the three of them would fly back to Israel. Feingold suggested that Helga might be interested in visiting some of the tourist sites in both Washington and New York City. Helga agreed enthusiastically, and so that was arranged.

As David and Helga were walking to David's car, he leaned

over and said, "Helga, I am really impressed and very proud of you. That was an excellent and professional briefing you put on in there. I could tell everyone was impressed!"

Helga said, "Thank you," and kissed David on the cheek.

David spent the rest of the day showing Helga the various government buildings, museums, and statues in the city. Helga was particularly impressed by buildings such as the White House, the Capitol, and the building that housed the Supreme Court. By evening, both agents were tired out from visiting so many tourist sites.

June 18, 1957
New York City, USA

THE NEXT DAY, David and Helga took an early morning express train on the Pennsylvania Railroad that brought them to New York in less than three hours. After checking in at their hotel, David began showing Helga some of the more famous tourist sites. He took her to the Statue of Liberty and to Ellis Island by ferry. Then he took her to the top of the Empire State Building, which absolutely amazed Helga. Tel Aviv had some tall multi-story buildings, but nothing that could even remotely compare with the Empire State Building. Because it was a clear sunny day, Helga was able to see a great distance from the top of that historic building. But if she looked straight down, it made her very uncomfortable, a common occurrence with tourists.

David then took her to the Guggenheim Art Museum and in the evening to the Metropolitan Opera House. It turned out that Helga was very interested in the various sites and was delighted at the background information that David provided.

David also took Helga to a couple of restaurants at lunch and dinner that specialized in food from foreign countries, which Helga had never tasted before.

For both David and Helga, it was a time to relax and pretend they were a couple of carefree tourists. They managed to forget for those few hours the mission that awaited them back in the Middle East.

June 19, 1957
New York City, USA

In the morning, the two agents toured some more. Then, in the middle of the afternoon, they took a cab to Idlewild International Airport, where they met Feingold for the flight back to Israel.

Feingold and the two agents once again embarked on the long overnight flight to Paris and then on to Tel Aviv. Not much was said on the flight, with all three agents either sleeping or busy with their own thoughts.

June 20, 1957
Tel Aviv, Israel
Ben Gurion International Airport

Arriving back in Israel, Feingold thanked David and Helga for their participation in the meeting at the Pentagon. He further added that there would probably be more activity for them soon, but that, for the time being, they could relax and wait for a summons. He added that he was very pleased with them both in the way they had handled the briefing in Washington. With that, Feingold bade them goodbye, and the two agents retired to the Mossad building where they shared an apartment.

7

June 21-25, 1957
Jerusalem, Israel
Mossad Residence & Mediterranean Beach

For the next five days, David and Helga relaxed as they waited for a summons from the Mossad. They went to the beach, swam, and sunbathed every morning. In the afternoons, they strolled around Jerusalem looking at little shops. In the evenings, Helga insisted on cooking their meals. To David's great surprise and delight, she was an excellent cook and introduced David to a number of Middle Eastern dishes, which he found to be delicious. They also talked at length about their individual backgrounds. However, by common unspoken consent, they stayed away from discussing any possible future plans. They both knew instinctively that danger lurked in that direction and that this was not the time to bring up any possible future plans. And then they snuggled together in bed and made love whenever they felt like it.

June 26, 1957
Jerusalem, Israel
Mossad Headquarters

As they knew it would, the phone call from the Mossad came early that morning. It requested their presence at 10 a.m., and that ended their brief holiday.

At the Mossad Headquarters, Feingold and Epstein awaited them in the usual conference room.

Manny Epstein greeted them in a joking manner by saying, “Well, you two lazy bums. We are not paying your salaries just so you can loaf. It’s time to put you two back to work.”

David and Helga laughed at that and then waited to hear what awaited them.

Feingold said, “It appears that the next step is to send you back into Egypt. We simply must get more hard information. Through a contact we have there, we managed to get a message to Abdul that you would be returning. I’m hoping that you can then contact that technician, Alex, and set up a communication link with him. You two will have to stay at Abdul’s house and keep a very low profile. David, you will carry a sum of money to give to Abdul. It’s possible you’ll have to remain there more than one day.”

David and Helga both nodded their understanding of the situation.

Feingold then added, “While you are there, it is possible that, if the construction of the site is close to being finished, some of the necessary lab equipment will be undergoing delivery. Now, if Alex can identify the kind of equipment being delivered, that might be an excellent clue as to what the Nazis are planning. So please keep that in mind.”

Feingold hesitated briefly, then continued.

“It has been arranged for the two of you to be taken back to the Egyptian coast tomorrow night. The same MTB and the same captain will drop you off at the same spot as the last time. You'll be carrying a tiny low-power transmitter, which you can use to get the MTB to come back and pick you up. Keep in mind that you should transmit the pickup message at least six hours before the actual pick-up in order to give the MTB time to travel from its home port. The transmitter frequency will be monitored twenty-four hours a day. It will be up to you to decide how many days you remain in Egypt, depending on circumstances. Any questions from either of you?"

Neither David nor Helga had any. Feingold and Epstein wished them good luck and safe travel, and the meeting ended.

The two agents set off for their apartment, knowing that the following night they would be facing danger once more.

June 27, 1957
Ashdod, Israel
Israeli Navy Base

David and Helga boarded the same MTB at 10 that night. They were greeted by Captain Levy, the same captain who had taken them to Egypt the previous times. He was a handsome man who looked like a pirate with his beard and a sardonic way of speaking.

Captain Levy greeted them with an interesting message.

He said, "You two are screwing up my love life with these all-night operations. What am I going to tell my wife? She thinks I'm out all night with another woman! And anyhow, what the hell are you doing going over to Egypt all the time? Haven't you anything better to do with your nights?"

The two agents got a good laugh out of the captain's remarks.

Then David said, "I'll tell you if you promise to keep your

mouth shut. We started a casino over there, and we have to go and pick up our winnings!"

All three got a good laugh at that remark.

Captain Levy said, "Once we get underway, I want to talk to you two about my share of those winnings from your casino."

This brought forth even more laughter.

With that, he turned and gave the order to cast off. Moving very quietly, the MTB eased out of the harbor. Once a few miles out, the captain set up a cruise speed of 25 knots and a course that would bring them near the spot where the two agents would disembark. Then the captain suggested that David and Helga take naps below decks until they got close to the Egyptian coast, which they did.

June 28, 1957
Mediterranean Sea
Egyptian Shore

Some hours later, the MTB arrived at the same spot as before, about a mile offshore from the Egyptian coast. The same two crew members took them ashore in an inflatable boat. But before they left the MTB, Captain Levy shook their hands and, with no trace of a smile, wished them luck and said he would be back to pick them up when they were ready to return. It was obvious the captain was well aware of the risk the two agents were taking going back into Egypt once again.

Once on the beach, David and Helga shouldered their heavy backpacks and, moving as quietly as possible, set off for the village located not far from the labs under construction. It appeared the Egyptian government was not particularly concerned about anyone making a landing on that stretch of coast.

However, after having hiked for about an hour, they were surprised to hear dogs barking in the distance. They stopped walking, and David wet a finger and held it up to get a better idea of the direction of the light breeze that was blowing. It was blowing toward the sea and also toward the sound of the dogs barking. David whispered, "We've got to find a hill and put it between us and the dogs!"

Helga whispered, "Do you see anything like that?"

They peered through the darkness, trying to spot any kind of small hill.

Then Helga whispered, "David, over there, a short distance looks like a hill!"

David agreed, and they quickly moved in that direction. Once behind the hill and sheltered from the dogs, they crouched down. Helga whispered, "I sure hope those dogs lost our scent!"

Both agents had pulled out small revolvers in case they needed to protect themselves against the patrol and its dogs. But a short time later, the dogs stopped barking as they lost the scent. David and Helga remained crouched down for another twenty minutes, but after not hearing any more sounds, they crept from behind the small hill and slowly and carefully set off again.

David said very quietly, "Whew, that was a close call."

Helga agreed.

Sunrise found them lying hidden behind another small hill near the village. By morning, when the village was stirring and many people were walking around, they walked casually to the village and to Abdul's small house.

At Abdul's house, his wife, Deborah, greeted them with a warm smile.

She suggested they rest while she cooked a simple but tasty breakfast for them. Deborah worked part-time as a teacher at the village school and spoke fluent English. She told the agents that Abdul would be home for a midday meal around noon. Abdul and Deborah had two small children, and the agents spent the rest of the morning relaxing in a shaded outdoor area, chatting with Deborah and watching the children playing.

As promised, around noon, Abdul arrived and greeted them. After giving his wife some groceries from their store, he sat with the agents while Deborah cooked a meal. David gave Abdul the money that the Mossad had requested that they deliver to him. Abdul accepted the funds gratefully. After the meal was finished, Abdul sat down with the agents to find out what he could do to further their mission. David mentioned that they definitely needed to meet with Alex, and Abdul said it was likely that Alex's wife would visit the grocery store in a day or two, as she normally did. Through her, Abdul could get a message to Alex.

Abdul said he thought that it was likely Alex would appear within a couple of days. David also asked whether there had been any indication that the labs were close to completion. Abdul mentioned that based on his grocery business, it appeared more personnel were being hired for the labs. David considered that to be an important piece of information, and Helga agreed.

While the two agents waited for Alex to appear, they stayed out of sight. Abdul had a small storage shed behind his house, and it was there that the two agents slept.

June 30, 1957
Village Near Labs, Egypt
Abdul's House

FORTY-EIGHT HOURS PASSED before Abdul saw Alex's wife in the village and was able to pass on to her the fact that two Mossad agents were at Abdul's house and wanted to meet with Alex. Late that evening, Alex showed up at Abdul's house. Abdul introduced him to David and Helga. Deborah served coffee and sweets to everyone and then sat quietly in a corner. Abdul and Alex were totally different physically. Abdul was of medium height and had somewhat dark skin, while Alex was considerably taller and had lighter skin coloring.

The meeting was initially awkward because it was obvious that Alex was fearful that the meeting might be a trap set up by the Nazis. When David realized this, he decided to take a chance that Alex was indeed a friend.

David said, "Alex, you must have realized by now that Helga and I are working for the State of Israel. This project that the Nazis have dreamed up has a lot of people very worried. Our job is to find out what exactly that project is. Helga and I are hoping you may be willing to help us in that mission."

Alex said, "I had not realized initially what this project was about and who was likely to be involved. Now I cannot leave the project without endangering my life and the lives of my family, so I hope you will keep this in mind."

David reassured him by saying, "We'll do our best to protect both you and your family, and we can probably get all of you to either Israel or America if that is your wish. But in the meantime, we would like to get as much information as possible about the labs. However, we most certainly do not want to endanger your life. So we'll have to set up some way for you to get info to us safely. In the meantime, I have a few questions that maybe you can answer."

Alex said. "I'm really grateful for anything you can do to protect myself and my family."

Helga asked, "What is it that you are supposed to be doing at the labs?"

Alex answered, "Currently, they are using me to do two things. I'm supposed to oversee the construction and outfitting of some of the labs. I am also supposed to expedite the delivery of equipment for the labs."

Helga said, "Interesting. How soon do you think the labs will be ready to begin functioning?"

Alex said, "I'm not sure, but my guess is in six to eight weeks and maybe longer!"

David looked at Helga and raised his eyebrows as if to say, "That's not a lot of time!"

Helga said, "Alex, we need to get as much information as possible in the next few weeks. Can you tell us anything about the equipment being delivered to the labs?"

Alex answered, "Yes, I can tell you about one type of equipment that is arriving in very large quantities, and that's centrifuges. These are large centrifuges, and I've never heard of a lab needing so many of them. Every few days, we get another shipment of them. I really don't understand what that is all about, but maybe someone back in Israel may have a clue."

David asked, "Is the security there very tight?"

Alex answered, "Oh, yes, that pig Rochman has guards all over the place as well as spies. I'm going to have to be very careful not to get caught."

David said, "Alex, believe me, we don't want either you or Abdul to get caught. Would it be better in the future if you did not come here at all except in a real emergency? Maybe when you or your wife goes to Abdul's store, she can slip him written messages?"

Alex and Abdul both thought that might be a good idea, but that, for the time being, they would meet with David and Helga in person.

David said, "Alex, here is some money to help you and your wife. And Abdul, both you and Alex should let me know if you need more. But please be very careful how you spend this money. If the security people catch on that either of you has a sudden influx of funds, they are very likely to become suspicious."

Abdul nodded, and Alex said, "Yes, I understand, and my wife and I will be very careful."

Both Egyptians thanked David profusely.

Then David asked, "Abdul, how do you get messages to the Mossad now?"

Abdul answered, "I mail messages to someone I've never met at the British Embassy in Cairo, who then passes them on to the Mossad. But I don't know how long they will be willing to continue doing that. If the Egyptian Government catches them doing it, they will probably be forced to return to England."

Helga said thoughtfully, "We may have to find another way to pass on information."

David then asked, "Alex, is there anything else that you saw being delivered that might be a clue as to what those Nazis are planning?"

Alex answered, "Yes, there is something else. There have been shipments of some kind of gas that comes in steel cylinders similar to oxygen cylinders. But I have a feeling it's not oxygen in those cylinders."

David said, "That could be another important clue. We'll have to see what the scientists back in Israel make of all this."

Shortly thereafter, Alex quietly left after promising David and Helga that he would pass on any kind of information he could gather to Abdul.

Helga asked Abdul if he felt that he was under any kind of surveillance by the security people at the lab or by Egyptian intelligence. Abdul answered that he didn't think so, but that it was very difficult to be sure.

Late that evening, David sent the radio message that told the MTB captain they would be ready to be picked up later that night. Then David and Helga bid Abdul and Deborah goodbye and set off on the hike to the shore. Once again, they walked carefully and quietly without speaking for fear that a passing security patrol might overhear them.

They reached the shore without incident and sat down

on the sand to wait for the arrival of the MTB. They kept a sharp lookout for any patrols and talked very quietly. Almost two hours later, the same inflatable that had dropped them off appeared out of the dark night. The two agents climbed aboard without saying a word and eventually got back aboard the MTB. Captain Levy greeted them and suggested they get below and rest.

After reaching the MTB's home port in Ashdod in the early morning, the two agents returned home and went to sleep.

July 2, 1957
Cairo, Egypt
President's Nasser Villa

ON THAT DAY, President Nasser had contacted the three Nazi Colonels and had requested their presence at his villa for a meeting. When they arrived, President Nasser, as usual, chaired the meeting and immediately got down to business. He asked the two scientists if they had been able to determine the best way to proceed toward the goal of destroying Israel.

Dr. Schweitz, the specialist in nuclear science and the one who tended to take the lead, spoke up first.

He said, "Mr. President, Dr. Reicher and I have consulted at length about the best and most destructive approach. We believe it should be a two-prong approach. My staff will manufacture a sufficient number of small rockets that have nuclear warheads. These warheads, rather than causing huge explosions, will cause smaller explosions that will release large quantities of radiation in sufficient quantities to quickly kill large numbers of people. Dr. Reicher, using the gas formula he invented during World War II, has designed a small rocket that disperses his poison gas at low altitudes. We believe the double attack should exterminate between ninety and ninety-five percent of the entire population of Israel!"

Schweitz stopped talking, and he and the others waited for Nasser's reaction. After a few seconds, a broad smile illuminated Nasser's face. He positively glowed.

He said, "Magnificent, gentlemen! If you can really make this happen, you will go down in history as the saviors of mankind!"

At that, the two Nazi scientists smiled in appreciation of Nasser's rather extreme compliments. They did not realize that if the 'Sword of Damocles' project were to succeed, they would go down in history as the greatest killers of all time, particularly since the two-prong attack would almost certainly kill many more people outside of Israel.

Nasser then turned to Colonel Rochman and asked, "And you, Colonel, are you satisfied with the current security arrangements?"

Rochman thought for a few seconds and then said, "Mr. President, once the entire building is completed and the construction crews are gone, it will be possible to institute much tighter security measures. In the meantime, I have requested that patrols be increased in that area as well as along the Mediterranean shore. I believe that should suffice. I really do not believe the Israelis are capable of penetrating our security. They are really not that smart!"

Again, Nasser smiled, showing his satisfaction.

Now, Nasser said, "I have given orders for the building contractors to finish their work as soon as possible. And I am seeing to it that the story is spread widely that this building is being built to house a new and revolutionary method for making textiles. That should explain the tight security!"

The three Nazi Colonels all nodded their agreement at Nasser's rather grandiose statements.

With that, the meeting ended, and the three Nazis departed.

July 6, 1957
Jerusalem, Israel
Mossad Headquarters

RETURNING FROM THEIR incursion into Egypt, the two agents prepared a report of their trip to Egypt, which Helga dropped off at the Mossad Headquarters.

After four days, during which David and Helga heard nothing from the Mossad, they were eventually summoned to the Mossad Headquarters that morning by a phone call. In the days since their return from Egypt, David and Helga had relaxed and, more importantly, had gotten to know each other much better. The two exchanged stories about their early years, their families, and more. Helga, in particular, talked about her time in Treblinka, a memory that brought tears to her eyes. David encouraged her to talk about her experiences not only at Treblinka but also afterwards during the escape and the long trip to Turkey. David believed that for Helga, unburdening herself of those memories was a good catharsis. It brought them much closer to each other. But this period of mutual discovery ended with the message from the Mossad.

Arriving at the Headquarters, they met with both Feingold and Epstein.

When they entered the conference room, both agents sensed an air of urgency. Feingold and Epstein seemed preoccupied and tense.

Feingold began the meeting and said, "We have received information that tells us President Nasser met with the three Nazi Colonels a few days ago. The informant said that at the meeting, Nasser and the Colonels arrived at a specific strategy. In addition, it was decided to increase the security in the area. This is not good news. We believe the time has come to try to create a better connection with the man you call Alex. That means you two will have to go back into Egypt. I don't like sending you two back in so soon, especially with the increased security, but there doesn't seem to be much of a choice. Helga, how do you feel about going back in?"

Helga hesitated for a split second, looked at David, then said, "Mr. Director, I don't see that there is any choice either. I think we are both ready to go back to Egypt and to try and set up a much better connection with Alex."

David merely nodded his agreement.

Epstein spoke for the first time and asked, "Do you two feel that putting you ashore at night is a reasonably safe way to get you back in?"

David said, "It seems to be the quickest and best way, and we don't have a lot of time to waste!"

Helga said, "Yes, I agree with David".

Then Epstein came up with a brilliant idea.

He said, "I remember you saying that shore patrols always seem to have dogs with them. The Mossad perfected a spray that, when used, will greatly reduce the ability of any dog to detect the scent of a human being. I'll make sure you are equipped with some spray bottles of that spray."

Helga said, "Manny, that could be a real help if we come across any of those patrols!"

With that settled, it was agreed by all that thirty-six hours later, the two agents would be ferried by the usual MTB to the coast of Egypt. Once again, their cover story would be that they were amateur archeologists searching for likely archeological sites in case they were caught and questioned by security forces.

The meeting ended on a somber note as the two agents understood that each time they entered Egypt, their danger increased.

July 7, 1957
Ashdod, Israel
Israeli Navy Base

As before, the two agents boarded the same MTB of the Israeli Navy in the early evening. Captain Levy greeted them and suggested they go below and rest until it was time to disembark and take the small inflatable to the Egyptian shore. David and Helga lay close together on a bunk, not saying anything. After a while, David drew Helga close and they huddled together, eventually dozing off. Some time later, Captain Levy came below and woke them. He suggested they eat something before disembarking, which they did. Then it was time to get back aboard the same small inflatable. The two crewmen rowed them quietly toward shore, but when they were still a considerable distance from the beach, they suddenly heard the sound of two dogs barking. The two crewmen immediately turned the inflatable around and rowed further offshore, hoping the dogs would not be able to pick up their scent. Eventually, the barking stopped, and it seemed that the patrol had moved off. Nevertheless, the crewmen sat and waited patiently without making any attempt to reach shore. The four occupants of the inflatable remained totally silent. After a full thirty minutes of drifting silently, the crewmen finally resumed rowing toward shore.

Once ashore, David and Helga waved goodbye to the two crew members and lost no time silently setting off for the village and Abdul's house.

They walked more silently and carefully than ever before, realizing that the security in the general area of the labs had probably been increased. They frequently stopped their walking to listen for any voices or dogs barking. However, they heard nothing.

July 8, 1957
Village Near Labs, Egypt
Abdul's House

JUST BEFORE SUNRISE, the two agents reached Abdul's small house. Not wishing to disturb the family at that early hour, they crept into Abdul's storage shed behind the house and lay down for a couple of hours. Then they softly knocked on the back door, which was opened by Abdul himself. He greeted them warmly, as did his wife Deborah, and they all sat down to breakfast.

David eventually asked Abdul when he thought Alex might show up. Abdul thought Alex's wife might be coming to his grocery store that day, in which case it would be possible for Alex to show up that evening.

When Abdul came home for the midday siesta, he informed the two agents that Alex's wife had, in fact, shown up at the store that morning, and that it was likely Alex would make an appearance that evening. David and Helga rested during the day and spent time with Deborah, waiting for the evening. That evening, Alex did show up, and the two agents were greatly relieved.

After Deborah served coffee, David decided to initiate the topic of the labs.

David said, "Alex, Helga and I are here because we are totally against what those three Nazi officers are planning on creating at the site under construction. How do you feel about those Nazis?"

Alex was silent for a few moments as he tried to frame his words carefully.

Finally, he said, "I have lived in Egypt all my life and am very unhappy about the current president, who is basically a dictator. My wife is Jewish, and I have been afraid for her ever since I married her. I also have two small children. Because of them, I may decide to try to move the entire family to either Israel or America as soon as I can save some money. That is why I am working in the labs. The Nazi officers scare me greatly. I am still not sure what they are planning, but I'm willing to bet it will be something terrible. They all seem to be crazy to me. And now that I have said that much, if you two are undercover agents for President Nasser, then I'm as good as dead already."

David laughed and said, "Alex, as we have told you, we work for the State of Israel. We do not work for Nasser. I actually work for the American government, but am on loan to Israel, and Helga works for the State of Israel. Do you mind if I ask you some personal questions about your background?"

Alex said he would not mind at all.

David asked Alex to briefly describe his background.

Alex gathered his thoughts and then responded, "I studied chemistry at Cairo University and then worked in a number of places as a chemist. The government put out a notice saying they were looking for various types of scientists and technicians for a project. I signed up not because I believed in any government project but because the pay was better than anywhere else in Egypt. I had no idea I would be working for a group of Nazis, and it was a good thing that when they hired me, they did not know my wife was Jewish!"

Helga said forcefully, "You don't know how lucky you were!"

David said, "Alex, as I have told you before, Helga and I will do everything in our power to protect you and your family!"

Alex said. "I'm really grateful for anything you can do in that regard."

David looked at Helga, who had sat silently up to now.

Now Helga spoke up, saying, "Alex, we need to get as much information as possible in the next few weeks, so we hope you'll be able to find out more as to what is going on at those labs."

David added, "Alex, believe me, we don't want either you or

Abdul to get caught. Would it be better if, in the future, you did not come here at all except in a real emergency? Maybe when you or your wife go to Abdul's store, you can slip him written messages?"

Alex and Abdul both thought that was a good idea and would plan on passing information in that way.

David said, "Alex, here is some money to help you and your wife. And Abdul, both you and Alex should let me know if you need more."

Both Egyptians thanked David gratefully.

Then David asked, "Abdul, how do you get messages to the Mossad now?"

Abdul answered, "I mail messages to someone I've never met at the British Embassy who then passes them on to the Mossad."

David then asked, "Alex, is there anything else that you saw being delivered that might be a clue as to what those Nazis are planning?"

Alex answered, "Yes, there is something else. There have been shipments of some kind of gas that comes in steel cylinders similar to oxygen cylinders. But I have a feeling it's not oxygen in those cylinders."

David said, "That could be another important clue. We'll have to see what the scientists back in Israel make of all this."

Shortly thereafter, Alex quietly left after promising David and Helga that he would pass on to Abdul any kind of information he could gather.

Helga asked Abdul if he felt that he was under any kind of surveillance by the security people at the lab or by Egyptian intelligence. Abdul answered that he didn't think so, but that it was very difficult to be sure.

David sent the required message to the MTB that indicated they were ready to be picked up later that night.

Later that evening, David and Helga bid goodbye to Abdul

and his wife and set off for the Egyptian shore. After three hours of silent and careful walking under the moonlight, they were close to the Mediterranean shore when they suddenly heard the sound of dogs barking not far away.

Helga whispered, "We've got to get behind a hill, quick!"

Looking around, they spotted a small hill not far away. Moving as quietly as possible, they crouched down on the far side of the hill, thus putting it between themselves and the security patrol. The dogs, losing the scent, stopped barking. David and Helga remained behind the small hill for some time, listening intently in case the security patrol came around to the far side of the hill. But there was no sound of any kind. Evidently, the patrol had moved off.

After some twenty minutes, they resumed their walk toward the beach. Using the short-range low-power transmitter he had been issued, David sent a message to the MTB lying offshore. The signal also helped Captain Levy pinpoint exactly where the two agents were on the beach. Not long after reaching the beach, the inflatable could be seen approaching. Just then, they heard the sound of dogs barking again. Helga whispered, "Quick, into the water!"

The two agents entered the water as quietly as possible and moved toward the inflatable. With some help, they got aboard the inflatable, and the crewmen paddled silently toward the waiting MTB.

Soon, the agents were back aboard the MTB, where Captain Levy welcomed them. Levy said, "I thought I heard the sound of dogs barking, but it was very faint."

Helga said, "You did hear dogs. We had to hide behind a hill to avoid that patrol! And then we heard dogs barking again, and we walked into the sea to meet your inflatable further offshore!"

Levy said, "It seems that putting you on shore and picking

you up again is getting more dangerous. I think we all need to be very careful if there are any more trips like this one!"

David said, in a very heartfelt tone of voice, "You'd better believe it."

July 13, 1957
Jerusalem, Israel
Mossad Headquarters

AFTER A NUMBER OF DAYS during which David and Helga heard nothing from the Mossad, they were eventually summoned to the Mossad Headquarters that morning by a phone call. In the previous few days since their return from Egypt, David and Helga had relaxed and, more importantly, had gotten to know each other much better. The two exchanged stories about their early years, their adulthood, their families, and more. It brought them much closer together. But this period of mutual discovery ended abruptly with the message from the Mossad.

Arriving at the Headquarters, they met with both Feingold and Epstein.

When they entered the conference room, David sensed an air of urgency. Both Feingold and Epstein seemed preoccupied, and the morning greetings were brief.

Feingold began the meeting and said, "We have received information that tells us President Nasser met with the two Nazi scientists a few days ago. It leads us to believe that at the meeting, the three arrived at a specific strategy. We also believe the time has come to try to create a better connection with the man you call Alex. This would be the fourth time you enter Egypt at night with the MTB, leaving you on the beach. The last time you almost ran into a patrol with dogs. I don't like sending you back in so soon one little bit, but there doesn't seem to be much of a choice. Helga, how do you feel about going back in?"

Helga hesitated for a split second, looked at David, then said, "Mr. Director, I don't see that there is any choice either. I think we are both ready to go back to Egypt and to try to set up a much better connection with Alex. I do think that David and I will have to be extra cautious. That patrol with dogs may be a sign that the security anywhere close to the labs has been increased."

David nodded his agreement.

Then David said, "Based on what Alex told us this last time, it seems to me that the labs may be getting close to beginning their real work."

Epstein spoke for the first time and asked, "Do you two feel that putting you ashore at night is a reasonably safe way to insert you into Egypt?"

David said, "It seems to me the quickest and best way, and we don't seem to have a lot of time to waste."

Helga said, "Yes, I agree with David."

Epstein said, "Then I guess that settles it, but I still don't like sending you two back in so soon!"

Then Feingold spoke up and said, "There is one thing we can do to make this next insertion into Egypt somewhat safer. I talked to someone at the Israeli Navy Headquarters, and on this next trip, there will be a second MTB assigned. This second MTB will move along the Egyptian coast and will get very close to the shore at a point well West of Alexandria. This MTB will act as a decoy and a distraction, and hopefully make it easier and safer for you two to get ashore and make it to the village safely. What do you two think about the diversion?"

David and Helga looked at each other and then both nodded.

Helga said, "Yes, that might draw any possible attention away from us. Thank you for thinking of this idea, Mr. Feingold!"

Feingold said, "You two are very important to us and we have to try and protect you both to the greatest extent possible!"

With that settled, it was agreed by all that thirty-six hours later, they would be ferried by the same MTB to the coast of Egypt. Once again, their cover story would be that they were archeologists in case they were caught and questioned by security forces.

July 14, 1957
Ashdod, Israel
Israeli Navy Base

As before, the two agents boarded the same MTB of the Israeli Navy in the early evening. Captain Levy greeted them and suggested they go below and rest until it was time to disembark and take the small inflatable to the Egyptian shore. David and Helga lay close together on a bunk, not saying anything. After a while, David drew Helga close, and they huddled together, eventually dozing off.

July 15, 1956
Egyptian Shore
Early Morning

Some time later, Captain Levy came below and woke them up. He suggested they eat something before disembarking, which they did.

Before leaving the MTB, Captain Levy took them aside.

Captain Levy said, "I've been briefed about the other MTB that is going to act as a decoy. You may hear its engines as you are rowed to shore. I sure hope it will distract the Egyptians. Look, I know about the patrol you almost ran into the last time I brought you here. I warned the two crewmen who are going to row you to the beach to be extra careful and take all the time they need to make sure there is no patrol anywhere close by! I'm going to take the MTB further away this time because I'm worried that if the Egyptian radar spots me sitting a few miles offshore, it might give the game away. So, you might want to send me the pickup message while you are still a long way from the beach. Then send it again when you reach the beach."

Helga said, "Thank you, Captain. David and I really appreciate all you are doing to ensure our safe journey."

The captain replied, "I haven't been told what's going on, and I'm not asking. All I know is it must be damn important! You two certainly have guts. Well, I'll be waiting at some distance offshore for you to be ready to be picked up. Travel safe!"

Helga said, "Thank you, Captain."

David and Helga shook hands with the captain and boarded the inflatable.

The trip to the beach was more silent than ever as the two crewmen paddled. As they were approaching the shore, they heard the far-off sounds of marine engines and knew they belonged to the other MTB moving along the coast. Once having safely reached the shore, they were bid a whispered goodbye, and the inflatable disappeared in the darkness on its way back to the MTB.

July 15, 1957
Village Near Labs
Abdul's House

David and Helga walked slowly and very quietly inland about three miles and then lay down on the sand to wait for daybreak.

Even more than on the previous trips, they felt danger acutely. They remained awake and alert, listening for the sound of any patrolling guards. Eventually, sunrise came, and they looked around for guards, but none were in sight. They resumed their trek to the small village where Abdul and his family lived. After some more hiking, they eventually reached the still slumbering village and went directly to Abdul's small house, where they were greeted like old friends.

Abdul was still at home since it was too early to open his grocery store. David and Helga both wanted to talk to Abdul that morning before he left for the store, and so the three got together immediately.

David began by saying, "Abdul, I think it is only fair to warn you that from now on, you and your family are in greater danger from the security people at the labs. So, when we come here, we will have to remain indoors during the day. Here is more Egyptian currency for you, but I must warn you again about spending it too freely. That could easily attract the attention of the security people."

Abdul nodded his understanding of the situation.

David continued, "Also, we urgently need to meet with Alex. If he or his wife comes into your store or if you can safely contact him, we need to meet with him. I will leave it to you and Alex to decide where and when to meet. But try to make it soon. In the meantime, I'm afraid Helga and I will have to impose on you and your wife and remain here indoors."

Abdul said, "David, that is understood, and my wife understands also. Thank you for the money you have brought me, and I will be very careful and use it sparingly, if at all. As to Alex, I believe it would be better if we wait for him or his wife to come to the store. When either comes, I will pass on your urgent request for a meeting. Until then, you will have to stay indoors in the daytime. After nightfall, you can probably sit outdoors unless it becomes too chilly."

For the rest of that day, David and Helga spent the time chatting with Abdul's wife and resting. Much to David's surprise,

Helga proved to be very comfortable playing with Abdul's children. She also became very friendly with Abdul's wife.

That evening after supper, David and Helga sat outdoors relishing the cooling air and talking very quietly for fear that anyone passing by might hear them.

July 16-17, 1957
Village near Labs
Abdul's House

For the next thirty-six hours, the two agents had to control their impatience and wait for Alex or his wife to appear at the grocery store. That evening, as soon as he got home, Abdul advised them that in a couple of hours, Alex should appear. When he did, David and Helga greeted him warmly, and together with Abdul, the foursome sat down to discuss the situation.

David felt he should begin the meeting. He said, "Alex, thank you for coming tonight. I know it isn't easy for you to come here without possibly alerting security. I want you to know that the information you are providing is extremely important. However, there have been indications recently that the security around the labs is being increased. Have you noticed that?"

Alex answered, "Yes, I certainly have seen signs of increased security. Everyone working there has noticed it also."

David said, "I think the first thing we need to do tonight is to figure out a way for you Alex to transmit information to Abdul with a minimum of risk to either of you. Do either of you have any suggestions?"

Everyone was silent for a couple of minutes. Then Alex said, "The best way may be if my wife passes information on to Abdul when she goes to do her grocery shopping. That shouldn't arouse any suspicion."

David said, "That makes sense, Alex. Do you think she will mind?"

Alex said, "David, my wife is extremely worried about what this whole Nazi project could mean for Israel. So I can guarantee she will be more than willing to help any way she can!"

With that settled, David went on to the next problem facing Helga and himself.

David said, " We need to find a safe way for Abdul to get the information to us. We cannot continue to come here because sooner or later, we could easily be caught. At the moment, I can't think of a way to do this."

Once again, the room became silent as all four participants thought about the problem.

Finally, Abdul said hesitantly, "What if my family and I drove to the shore, say every Sunday. We could leave a written message in a particular spot under a rock. Then maybe one of the Israeli Navy torpedo boats could pick up the message that night. It is so hot at this time of the year that it is not uncommon for families to go to the beach. Also, it is a perfect place for the children to play."

David looked at Helga and asked, "What do you think, Helga?"

After a few seconds, Helga responded, "I can't think of any better way."

David asked, "How will we know where the spot is so that we can tell the torpedo boat captain?"

Abdul said, "If I come with you tonight, I know of a spot that is near where you have come ashore in all your past trips."

David and Helga thought that was an excellent idea.

Helga said, "Now that's settled, Alex, do you have any additional information as to what is happening at the labs?"

Alex responded, "I can tell you that the two Nazi scientists are pushing the construction just as hard as they can. All kinds of equipment are arriving daily. The basic building is almost finished. A lot of centrifuges are still coming in. I understand these are needed for what appears to be one half of the entire project and relates to nuclear weapons. I will try to have more solid information in a couple of weeks, but I have to be very careful about asking too many questions. The two Nazi scientists and the other colonel are very suspicious!"

Alex took a deep breath and then continued.

Alex said, "There are rumors among the staff that a schedule has been created. I have not seen it, but I imagine we'll be told about it sooner or later. In the meantime, the Nazi scientists are putting a lot of pressure on the building contractor to finish the job. In fact, additional construction workers have been brought in. Also, some German technicians were added to the staff to begin the work of building the two different kinds of weapons. I think that in the next few weeks I'll know a lot more about these weapons. As soon as I do, I'll pass the information to Abdul. In fact, I'll try to have my wife give an update to Abdul at the store each week."

Helga said, "Alex, David and I are very worried about your safety. You are going to have to be extremely careful from now on."

Alex nodded his head in agreement.

David asked, "Alex, have you told your wife more about any of this?"

Alex responded, "Yes, she knows everything. She is horrified at what these Nazis seem to be planning. I met my wife at Cairo University. Her mother was originally from Great Britain and was working in the British Embassy. She met an Egyptian diplomat, and they fell in love and married. My wife would like to immigrate to Israel or the U.S. at some point, and so would I!"

Helga said, "Now I understand your motivation for helping us in spite of the danger!"

Shortly thereafter, Alex bid everyone good night and left.

Abdul then suggested they wait an hour or so, and then he would lead them to the spot on the shore that he had in mind.

After Alex left, David sent off the short message to the MTB alerting Captain Levy that they would be ready to be picked up later that night. An hour later, Helga and David bid Abdul's wife goodbye and, together with Abdul, set off for the Mediterranean shore. Abdul had suggested first going to the spot where the agents usually came ashore, so that he could show them where the other location was in relation to where the agents had been dropped off previously.

The three walked under a bright moonlight, listening for any sounds of a security patrol. There was no talking among them for fear of betraying their presence. After three hours of steady hiking, they reached what David thought was approximately where they had been put ashore. Alex then led them about a half a mile away, where the beach had some rock formations near the water.

Abdul whispered, "I think this might be a good location to hide messages between the rocks at the top."

David and Helga agreed.

Abdul asked, "Can you bring the MTB here tonight?"

David said that he thought so and told Abdul to leave and go home as quietly as possible. Abdul agreed, shook hands, and disappeared into the night.

David sent a very short radio message to the MTB lying well offshore. He gave the MTB the new approximate position where they would meet the inflatable. David and Helga then sat down, leaning back against the rock formation and huddling together.

Suddenly, they heard voices not far off, followed by the sound of dogs barking. The two agents realized that because they had been leaning against the rock formation, those same rocks had shielded them from the sound of the approaching patrol.

Helga whispered, "What do you think we should do?"

David whispered back, "They are too close for us to avoid them. Let's try to bribe them!"

Helga agreed, although somewhat hesitantly.

David said, "Follow my lead!"

With that, he stood up, walked around the rock formation, and as the patrol got close, greeted them in Arabic. Helga did the same.

One member of the patrol asked in a tough manner, "What are you two doing here in the middle of the night?"

David, speaking in a very polite tone, said, "Sir, please try to quiet your dogs, and I'll tell you."

The guard gave a command, and the dogs stopped barking.

Then David said, "Sir, this lady and I are in love. But she is married, and her husband won't give her up. This seems to be the only place we can meet. Please don't arrest us. If her husband finds out she's been seeing me, he'll try to get both of us killed. Please, sir, try and understand. And if you'll forget you ever saw us, I'll give you some money right now!"

The two guards both hesitated, while Helga embraced David and played the part of a frightened wife. David and Helga were both carrying silenced pistols in special holsters strapped to their backs, but did nothing to make the two guards more suspicious.

Eventually, the head guard said, "All right, let's see how much money you have!"

David said, "Yes sir, the money is right here in my knapsack!"

With that, he slipped out of his knapsack, laid it on the ground, and, moving slowly, opened it and took out a small bundle of Egyptian currency.

He gave the money to the head guard, and while the two

agents held their breaths, the guard counted it. Then he turned to David and said, "O.K., I'm going to let you two go. But you'd better not be here when I come back in a couple of hours!"

David and Helga both thanked him profusely and watched silently as the two-man patrol and its dogs moved off and disappeared.

David waited ten minutes, then pulled out the short-range radio and sent an urgent message to Captain Levy to hurry up and pick them up as soon as possible.

Some ninety minutes passed before they heard the distant muffled sound of the MTB's engines. Then those died, and shortly thereafter, the inflatable rowed by the two crewmen arrived.

David and Helga climbed aboard and, without a word being spoken, were rowed to the MTB. As they boarded the MTB, they heard the somewhat distant sound of the other MTB that had been dispatched as a decoy.

Once aboard their MTB, they quietly left the area heading for Israel. Captain Levy welcomed them back aboard but then complained, "Listen, you two, this isn't a special limousine service I run for VIPs. What the hell do you mean by telling me to hurry up to make the pick up? I think maybe I'll just dump you both overboard!"

Helga got down on her knees before the captain, and in a pleading tone said, "Your eminence, please don't throw us overboard! Please sir! Well, do anything you want, but don't throw us overboard!"

Some of the crew standing nearby burst out laughing, as did Captain Levy and the two agents.

David spent a few minutes briefing Captain Levy as to what had happened when they had been surprised by the shore patrol.

All Levy could say was, "Whew, I'm sure glad I have a nice, safe job on this MTB."

Then Levy said, "Listen, you two scoundrels, don't forget, from now on I'm to be addressed as 'Your Eminence!'"

This brought gales of laughter from everyone within hearing.

Levy then told them some hot soup awaited them below and turned to the job of conning the MTB.

The two agents were below in the small wardroom, gratefully eating some of the hick hot soup when they suddenly heard the sound of the engines die away.

David said, "Maybe we'd better go topside and see what is going on!"

Helga agreed, and the two agents climbed to the upper deck and looked around. They realized the crew was at action stations and was very quiet. They went forward to the small bridge and, speaking very softly, asked Captain Levy what was going on.

Levy said, "We spotted an Egyptian patrol boat out there. I think they may have heard our engines and are now looking for us. If shooting starts, you'd better lie flat on the deck!"

Just then, the sound of the Egyptian patrol boat's engines was heard coming closer, and then the beam of a very bright searchlight flashed out. The searchlight beam moved around and came close to the MTB. Captain Levy called to the crew manning the MTB's guns, "Stand by to commence firing!"

Then he called the engine room and said, "Engine room, be ready to give me full power!"

A moment later, the Egyptian searchlight beam found the MTB, and a voice rang out asking who they were.

Without waiting, Captain Levy gave the order, "Commence firing!"

Then he ordered the engine room to give him full power on the three engines.

The night darkness was lit up by the bright flashes coming

from the muzzles of the 20 mm and 40 mm guns of the MTB reaching out to the Egyptian patrol craft.

As the MTB engines roared to life and the MTB began moving, the tracers from the guns could be seen hitting the Egyptian craft. The searchlight was shot out, and a few seconds later, as the MTB gunners found the range, fires began to spring up on the Egyptian craft. The Israeli gunners continued to pour rounds into the enemy boat, with some rounds hitting very close to the waterline. The Egyptian return fire faltered and died away as the onboard fires grew bigger. Then the Egyptian crew could be seen launching lifeboats and evacuating the craft.

Captain Levy called out, "Cease firing!" and he then turned the MTB toward Israel.

David and Helga had been lying flat on the main deck in response to Captain Levy's order. Now they scrambled erect. As the MTB sped away, they could see the Egyptian patrol craft still burning brightly.

The two agents climbed up to the small bridge where Captain Levy was busy making sure the MTB was on the correct course.

Helga accosted him and said, "Captain, you did a great job saving your boat and us!"

Captain Levy looked at Helga with David standing close by and said, "That's what I get paid to do!"

Then he turned back to conning the MTB, which was now rushing through the darkness at full speed.

David and Helga lay down again in the wardroom and tried to nap until they reached Ashdod Harbor. Before disembarking in Ashdod, they thanked Captain Levy again for the way he had handled the very dangerous situation that had developed when the Egyptian patrol craft had intercepted them.

Captain Levy merely shrugged his shoulders and said, "I was just doing my job. But I'm sure getting tired of hauling you two around and then having my wife accusing me of going out with another woman every time I haul you miserable clowns around! I've got a mind to start charging you two miserable clowns for all this service."

Helga got very close to Captain Levy and, in a falsetto yet sexy voice, said, "Your eminence, I'm yours for the taking just to show you how grateful we are!"

Everyone began laughing. David and Helga, now speaking in very serious tones, thanked Captain Levy once more and disembarked.

They returned to their apartment in Jerusalem and fell into a deep slumber.

8

July 18-21, 1957
Jerusalem, Israel
Mossad Residence

THE FOLLOWING DAY, DAVID AND HELGA PREPARED A report summarizing their trip to Egypt, and Helga delivered it to the Mossad Headquarters. David and Helga knew from past experience that now they had to wait to be contacted and to be told what the next part of their assignment would be.

Each day, they slept late, had a good breakfast, and then sat in their apartment until past 11:00 a.m. After that, if the weather was good, they went to the beach for two to three hours before returning home.

July 22, 1957
Jerusalem, Israel
Prime Minister's Conference Room

EVENTUALLY, THE SUMMONS came early that morning, but to their surprise, the two agents were told to report to the office of the Prime Minister. They had no idea what this indicated in terms of their mission and were very curious to find out.

When David and Helga were ushered into the Prime

Minister's conference room, they found a number of individuals there. In addition to Prime Minister David Ben Gurion, with his snow white mantle of hair, there were present Moshe Feingold, the Mossad Director; Manny Epstein, the Deputy Director for Middle East Operations; and an Israeli Defense Force officer who was not introduced.

Feingold introduced David and Helga to the Prime Minister, who welcomed them very graciously and offered them coffee and sweets. Then the Prime Minister began speaking.

"Miss Horowitz and Mr. Knox, I've been getting regular reports on what the two of you have been doing, and I want to personally tell you that the State of Israel is most grateful for your efforts."

David and Helga said nothing, merely inclined their heads as a way to say thank you to the Prime Minister.

Ben Gurion continued, "Aside from what you two have discovered about this project of President Nasser, other sources have told us a bit more. Nasser calls his project 'The Sword of Damocles' and hopes to totally destroy Israel if the project is successful. That in and of itself is frightening enough. But from what little we have learned about this insane 'Sword of Damocles' affair, our scientists have told me that what the Nazis are contemplating could easily do major damage to areas of the Middle East outside of Israel. The human toll overall could easily be almost unimaginable."

The Prime Minister paused, and it was obvious that he was emotionally affected by the mere thought of what might happen. Then he resumed the narrative again.

"Both President Eisenhower, with whom I have consulted, and I feel strongly that while Israel could easily destroy that fake hosiery mill tomorrow, it would accomplish nothing. Nasser would simply build a similar facility elsewhere and probably in a location where it would be far less accessible for us."

Again, the Prime Minister paused and took a sip of his coffee. No one said a word.

Then Ben Gurion continued.

"Furthermore, I am convinced that this laboratory building should not be destroyed unless we can first remove proof of what the project hopes to accomplish. Beyond that, we would like to bring out the three Nazi Colonels who are spearheading the project and have them stand trial for what they did in World War II. The names of those three are still on the list of War Criminals that the Allies still want to bring to justice."

Once again, Ben Gurion stopped talking to gather his thoughts.

Then he said, "So you see, destroying the 'Sword of Damocles,' or SOD, is not quite so simple. Destroy it we must. But the timing is absolutely critical. We cannot have the entire world condemn Israel as a rogue society that goes around destroying anything it wants to without reason!"

Now the Prime Minister stopped talking, drew a deep breath, and looked directly at David and Helga.

He said, "Mr. Knox and Miss Horowitz, I understand you two are not in the business of making major political or military decisions. On the other hand, you may have some insights that the rest of us are lacking. Would you have some ideas on how best to proceed?"

David looked at Helga, who simply smiled slightly and motioned with her hand for him to pick up the dialogue.

David said, "Prime Minister, this is indeed a very ticklish situation. I certainly don't have a ready answer. Might it be possible for Miss Horowitz and me to study the problem for two or three days and then report back to the Mossad?"

Ben Gurion replied, "Yes, we certainly have some time during which we can all try to reach some conclusions on how to proceed. Today is July 22. Do you think you might have some ideas to share by say July 28, five days from now?"

David again looked at Helga, who said, "Yes, that seems a good possibility, Prime Minister."

Ben Gurion looked at the others around the table, and everyone nodded their approval.

Ben Gurion then said, "Thank you all for attending today's meeting. Let's plan on meeting here on the 28th at 9 a.m."

With that, the meeting ended, although the Prime Minister took a minute to walk over to David and Helga and personally thanked them for their efforts to date.

July 22-27, 1957
Jerusalem, Israel
Mossad Headquarters

DURING THE FOLLOWING DAYS, David and Helga went each day to Helga's office at the Mossad Headquarters, trying to determine what the next step should be in the mission to destroy the 'Sword of Damocles' project of President Nasser. On the second day of their discussions, Helga brought up an important point.

Helga said, "David, you remember how the Prime Minister stressed the point that the State of Israel absolutely needs some hard proof as to what is being concocted in those labs. What if we could smuggle a mini camera to Alex? Maybe he could manage to take some really incriminating photos?"

David responded enthusiastically, "Helga, that's brilliant! Yes, that might be just what is needed! Let's recommend that when we meet on the 28th."

Then Helga said, "Yes, David, maybe the idea will be approved. But how do we get a mini camera to Abdul to pass on to Alex? Do we go in by MTB again? I feel that way may be increasingly risky."

David thought for a few moments and then said, "I agree with you, Helga. We could have the MTB leave the camera in those rocks where Abdul's messages are picked up. Or maybe another way might be to do what we did once before. Fly to Tunis and then Cairo and deliver the camera to Abdul's house. The problem is, how do we get the camera past Customs when we land in Cairo?"

Helga said, "That is a good question. Why don't we let the Mossad see if they can solve that problem?"

David agreed, and that's what they did.

July 28, 1957
Jerusalem, Israel
Prime Minister's Conference Room

ON THE 28TH, David and Helga arrived at the Prime Minister's suite of offices and were ushered into the conference room. Shortly, Feingold and Epstein arrived, followed by the Prime Minister. As before, Ben Gurion saw to it that everyone had coffee and sweets and then began the meeting. Ben Gurion looked at David and Helga and asked, "Have the two of you managed to come up with some strategy?"

David looked at Helga and said, "Go ahead."

Helga took a deep breath and began speaking.

She said, "Prime Minister and gentlemen, David and I clearly understand the need to obtain some kind of real proof as to what the labs are supposed to generate. What if we smuggled a mini camera to the man who is assisting us and who is currently employed at the labs? Would that be sufficient proof to show the world?"

There was silence for a few moments, and then the Prime Minister responded.

Ben Gurion said, "Yes, I think that would do very nicely.

That is an excellent idea! But how would you get the mini camera to that man?"

Helga said, "Prime Minister and gentlemen, David and I agree that continuing to penetrate Egypt by way of a motor torpedo boat could be increasingly dangerous. We feel it might be better to do what we did once before. We fly via commercial airline to Tunis and then Cairo. There is one problem, however, and that is how do we get the camera past Customs at the Cairo Airport?"

Epstein spoke for the first time and said, "I believe the Mossad can solve the problem of making the mini camera look like something else. Give me a few days to come up with an answer."

Ben Gurion said, "I think the whole approach is very feasible. Let us meet once more when the Mossad has solved the problem of hiding the camera. Thank you all for coming today, and I hope we can meet again very soon."

With that, the meeting ended on a positive note. As David and Helga prepared to leave the conference room, Manny Epstein came over and said, "Could you two secret agents find time in your busy and secret schedule to come to dinner tomorrow evening so that Esther won't threaten me with some terrible torture like putting me on a bread and water diet?"

David and Helga could not help laughing.

Helga said, "We were going to meet with President Nasser in Cairo tomorrow night for dinner, but we'll just have to tell him a prior engagement has come up. I'm sure he'll understand!"

Everyone got a good laugh over that, too.

July 29, 1957
Jerusalem, Israel
The Epstein Residence

WHEN DAVID AND HELGA arrived at the Epstein residence, they were met by Esther Epstein. She greeted them with a broad smile and a hug for each of them. Esther brought them into the living room, offered them a before-dinner drink, and apologized that Manny was not home yet from the office. Manny showed up shortly, and the foursome sat down to one of Esther's delicious dinners. The Epsteins kept the conversation light, and the time flew by. Over fruit and coffee, Esther turned to David and Helga with a twinkle in her eyes and said, "I have heard rumors that you two are romantically involved! Is there any truth to that?"

David and Helga looked at each other and burst out laughing.

Then David turned very serious and, in a quiet voice, said, "I can only speak for myself. The fact is that for the first time in my life, I feel that I am truly in love!"

With that, he stopped. Then he felt Helga's hand gripping his as she said, "I feel exactly the same way!"

Esther clapped her hands and exclaimed, "Wonderful!"

Manny joined in making it clear how he felt at the news.

Esther then proposed a toast to the couple.

She said, "May you reach a quiet part of your lives, marry, and have a great life! L'chaim!"

Then Esther said something that really surprised the two agents.

She said, "Manny and I have no children, partly because of our involvement in intelligence work. When the day comes, and I hope it will be soon, that you decide to marry, I wonder if you two would do Manny and myself the honor of letting us handle the wedding? It would mean a lot to us! And since neither of you have any family, it would give us a lot of joy to act on behalf of those who are no longer here!"

David and Helga were thunderstruck at the generosity and kindness of the offer. David started to say something and found himself so choked up he couldn't say anything. Helga sat there, and tears began trickling down her cheeks. There was total silence for a full three minutes. Finally, Manny said in a jocular tone, "Didn't mean to shake you two up. Esther, you've got to be more careful what you say!"

Finally, Helga managed to speak. She said, "Esther and Manny, that is such a wonderful offer that I think both David and I are really speechless. What a great offer! David, what do you think?"

Instead of answering, David stood up, went around the table, threw his arms around Esther, and kissed her on the cheek. Then he sat down again, still without saying a word. Helga did the same to first Manny and then to Esther, who then dabbed at her eyes as she also felt the emotion of the moment.

Manny suggested they all go back to the living room, where the conversation moved on to other subjects.

Just before they left the Epstein home, David said, "I don't see how Helga and I can think about anything other than the need to destroy this 'Sword of Damocles' insanity for the time being. Then we'll think about other things!"

Manny heartily agreed, as did Esther.

As David and Helga were getting ready to leave, David was finally able to express the emotion he felt.

"Esther and Manny, I want you both to know that for the first time in my life, I feel as if I have a family. I wonder if you realize what a gift you have given me!"

Helga chimed in, "I feel exactly the same way!"

On the way home, David and Helga could not stop talking about what a wonderful couple the Epsteins were.

July 30, 1957
Jerusalem, Israel
Mossad Headquarters

THAT MORNING, David and Helga had received a phone call requesting their presence at the Mossad Headquarters. When they arrived at the usual conference room, Manny Epstein was the only person present. He welcomed them and immediately got down to business. Manny had two identical large cameras sitting on the table in front of him. He waved them to chairs and began speaking.

Epstein said, "David and Helga, the Mossad technicians have solved the problem of how to hide the mini cameras. They took these two large cameras, altered the interiors, and created small compartments for the mini cameras. These cameras should get past the Egyptian Customs people without any trouble. As it happens, these types of large cameras that hide tiny mini cameras were developed by the British in World War II. Hopefully, you won't have any trouble getting into Egypt. What I don't know is whether Alex will have any difficulty carrying the mini cameras in and out of the labs. You'll have to discuss that with him when you meet."

"Moshe Feingold has briefed the Prime Minister on all of this, and he agreed that you should fly into Cairo as you did before via commercial airline. He also agreed there was no apparent reason to meet again at this time. He said to give you both his best wishes for safe travel and a successful trip. Mossad has bought two seats for you on a flight to Tunis, leaving tomorrow morning on a direct non-stop TWA flight to Tunis and then a second flight under different names for the leg from Tunis to Cairo, just as you did before. Any questions?"

David asked, "Why two cameras, Manny?"

Manny Epstein said, "Ah, yes, I was about to tell you. The last message from Abdul mentioned that Alex informed him that he thought he had found another employee who wants to help us."

David said, "I guess we don't have any questions. We'll be ready to go tomorrow. Wish us luck."

Epstein said, "You know we all wish you that. I hope this will work out. Travel safe. Call me as soon as you get back."

And with that, the meeting ended, and the two agents took the large, bulky cameras and returned home to prepare for their trip.

Aug. 1, 1957
Cairo, Egypt
Mossad Apartment

On that day, David and Helga duplicated the trip they had made weeks before. They flew by way of TWA to Tunis, Tunisia, switched passports, and then took another TWA flight to Cairo. Upon arriving at Cairo Airport, they passed through Customs with relatively little trouble. When they were questioned about the two large cameras they were carrying, David casually mentioned that they were so intrigued with the various Egyptian ruins that they wanted to take a lot of photos.

The Customs people appeared to be satisfied with David's explanations, and the agents heaved a breath of relief. But at Passport Control, a sharp-eyed employee began questioning them as to why they were returning to Cairo after having been there on May 15. David explained that they were very intrigued with the ancient Egyptian ruins, plus they were both amateur archeologists. The explanation seemed to satisfy the suspicious Passport Control agent, who decided they were a very rich American couple with nothing better to do than travel around and spend money. So David and Helga managed to legally enter Egypt. They took a cab to the apartment secretly owned by the Mossad, unpacked, and then went out for dinner. When they returned to the apartment, they called Abdul and, in a carefully worded manner, told him they were going to visit him the next day. Abdul indicated that it was fine and suggested they arrive around noon.

Aug. 2, 1957
Village Near Labs
Abdul's House

THE NEXT MORNING, there did not seem to be much choice as to what to do next. They got in the car that was kept there and headed for Abdul's house. When they got close to that house, they decided to park the car some distance away near a small mosque and then walked to Abdul's house. By doing this, they hoped to avoid attracting attention to Abdul and his family.

They knocked on the door, and Abdul's wife opened it. When she saw who was standing there, a broad smile lit up her face, and she embraced first Helga and then David. Once inside, Abdul joined them, and he too seemed very glad to see them.

The four of them sat down in the tiny living room, and David brought Abdul up to date, including the fact that he had parked the car at some distance. Abdul thought that was an excellent idea. David mentioned that they needed to reach Alex again. Abdul suggested that when Alex or his wife showed up at the grocery store, he would call David and, using a simple coded message, set up a meeting time. David and Helga agreed with the plan. Abdul had to leave so he could open his grocery store, but his wife asked the two agents to remain for a while and keep her company, which they did with pleasure. Later on, she served them a simple lunch, after which they walked back to the car and returned to the apartment in Cairo.

As expected, no call came that day or the next, which simply meant that neither Alex nor his wife had visited Abdul's grocery store.

Aug. 3, 1957
Village Near Labs
Abdul's House

Not surprisingly, David and Helga heard nothing until a call came from Abdul, which said that the following day, a Saturday, Alex would show up at Abdul's house at 11 a.m.

David and Helga drove out to the village and again left their car near the little mosque. They walked slowly to Abdul's house, and no one seemed to take any notice of them.

Abdul, his wife, and Alex greeted the agents with smiles, and they all sat down to discuss the situation. David gave Abdul and Alex each a packet of Egyptian money, which they accepted gratefully. Then David began briefing Abdul and Alex.

David said, "We still don't really know what the true goal of this whole operation is supposed to be or how it is to be achieved. I can tell you that destroying what is there now would be easy for Israel, but that is not Israel's overall goal. Helga and I have been told that the primary goal is to find out exactly what and how this project is supposed to work. A secondary goal is to capture the three Nazi colonels so they can stand trial rather than just to kill them. I also personally want to protect you two and your families. So, Alex, do you have anything new to report?"

Alex thought for a few seconds and then responded. He said, "From what little we've been told plus what I have seen with my own eyes, it appears that there are two weapons that will be developed, one nuclear and one some kind of poison gas. But it is not clear exactly how these weapons will be employed. I suspect that soon I will be directly involved only with the poison gas and will probably know nothing about the nuclear weapon. But I can tell you that manufacturing has not begun on either weapon."

The room was quiet for a minute as everyone thought about the problem.

Finally, David said, "Alex, is there any chance that there might be one other person who thinks like you and might help us unravel this whole mystery? Maybe someone in administration?"

Alex thought for a few moments and then answered, "Yes, there might be one individual. I don't know him very well. I'll try and see what his attitude his. A couple of times, he said things that made me think he is totally opposed to anything the Nazis try to do. But I have to be very careful because he might be someone planted there to catch someone like me. On the other hand, I've noticed the Nazi scientists seem very cocksure of themselves. It's almost as if they believe that nothing can possibly go wrong with their plan. That is their Achilles heel. They really seem to feel that no one can stop what they are planning."

David said, "Alex, how often do you see this other individual?"

Alex answered, 'I see him almost every day. We often sit together at lunch in the cafeteria."

Helga chimed in, "Alex, do you think you could very carefully try to find out how he really feels about the whole project?"

Alex said, "I'll try, but as I said, I have to be very careful!"

Helga said, "Absolutely! No question about that!"

Alex said, "If this other person seems to be someone we can trust, he will probably have to come here at night. It might be too dangerous for him to come in the daytime."

Everyone was in agreement on that point. There, the meeting ended since there didn't seem to be anything more to discuss. Alex said he would try to find out as much as he could about the person he often ate with and would pass any information on to Abdul.

Alex left Abdul's house and very carefully made his way

home. David and Helga left shortly thereafter and drove back to Cairo. While David drove, Helga kept checking the rear view mirror to see if they were being followed, but could not spot any vehicle trailing them.

Aug. 5, 1957
Cairo, Egypt
Mossad Apartment

DAVID AND HELGA tried hard to control their impatience as they waited to hear from Abdul. Eventually, the coded call from Abdul came, and that evening, David and Helga drove slowly and carefully to the little village and to Abdul's house. Since total darkness had already arrived, David decided to park the car behind the Abdul home. As before, Abdul's wife greeted them with a broad smile and ushered them into the small living room. Abdul and Alex were there together with a stranger. He was introduced as Omar, and everyone sat down. Omar spoke excellent English and appeared to be in his mid- or late 30s. He was of middle height with an open and honest face. To David's and Helga's surprise, Omar began the conversation.

He said, "Unless I am totally mistaken, all of you are concerned about what is going on at the labs where both Alex and I work. Well, so am I. I also understand that it is difficult for you to trust me. Please go ahead and ask any questions you may have."

David said, "Yes, we have some questions. For starters, could you tell us something about your background?"

Omar responded, "I'd be happy to. I was born in Cairo. My father was a physician. During World War II, I served in the British 8th Army and fought in North Africa and in Italy. In Italy, I was wounded and was hospitalized here in Cairo. There I met and later married a British nurse who was serving in that hospital. After I recovered, I went to Cairo University and studied physics, worked in a couple of places, and then came to work at the labs where I met Alex. And that's the short version of my life."

Helga asked, "Do you and your wife have any children?"

Omar smiled and said, "My wife is pregnant with our first child."

David asked, "What do you think of the work that is supposed to go on in that building?"

Omar said, "It is pretty obvious that the building is not a hosiery textile mill at all. The lower levels are for something entirely different. I have discussed this with Alex. Neither of us realized what we were getting into when we applied to work there. And we did not know that the entire project was in the hands of Nazi scientists. Now, if I wanted to leave the project, it might be very dangerous for both myself and my wife. So, you see, I am in a very difficult position. Also, I don't know who you are and whether you pose a threat to me.".

With that, Omar stopped talking and waited to see what would happen next.

David asked, "Why does the fact that the project is managed by Nazi scientists bother you so much?"

Omar responded, "A couple of years ago, I traveled in Europe. I took the time to visit one of the Nazi Execution camps, which is open to visitors. Does that answer your question?"

David looked at Helga but said nothing. The room was silent for a couple of minutes. Finally, Omar spoke again.

He said, "I realize the difficult position all of you are in. If you are who I think you are, maybe you can contact the British Embassy here and get a copy of my military file. Possibly that will help."

David said, "Not a bad idea. Thanks for thinking of that. I don't believe we can accomplish anything more tonight. Omar, if Alex suggests coming back here again in a few days, do you think you can make it?"

Omar said, "Absolutely!! Just let Alex know."

With that, the meeting ended, and Alex and Omar left shortly thereafter.

When David, Helga, and Abdul were alone, Abdul asked, "What do you think, David? Do you think Omar is on the level?"

David answered, "Possibly, maybe even probably. But I'll know more after I read his military file and see an original photo of him."

David wrote a short message requesting the Mossad to obtain a copy of Omar's military file from the British military records office, together with an original photo of him. David also asked that the file and photo be mailed directly to Abdul at his home, disguised as a memo from a company that sold groceries to grocery markets.

Then David said, "I'll radio the proper people tonight to have an MTB pick up my message tomorrow night. So Abdul, if you can drop off my message at the beach rocks tomorrow, and then we'll have to wait to see what the British Embassy here in Cairo sends you."

With that all arranged, David and Helga left and drove slowly back to the Cairo apartment where they were hiding out. Now they would have to wait for Abdul to contact them.

Aug. 6-10, 1957
Cairo, Egypt
Mossad Apartment

During the next four days, David and Helga had little to do as they awaited Abdul's call with the news he had received regarding the information David had requested about Omar. So, with time on their hands, they decided they might as well pretend to be tourists. They visited the part of Cairo that tourists usually visit. They also drove out to visit the Pyramids, the Sphinx, and also went to the Suez Canal and idly watched the busy canal traffic going by.

On the fifth day of their forced wait, they received a phone call from Abdul asking that they come by his house on Saturday evening. David decided to put the two large cameras in the trunk of their small car so they would be available if he and Helga decided they could trust not only Alex but also Omar.

Aug. 11, 1957
Cairo, Egypt
Abdul's House

THAT EVENING, the two agents drove carefully to Abdul's house. There, they found Alex and Omar had already arrived. In addition, the Mossad had managed to obtain a copy of Omar's military file and had gotten it to Abdul in record time.

While the others idly chatted, David scanned the file and then compared the photo of Omar to Omar himself, who was sitting near David.

Then David said, "Omar, your file and photo appear to show that everything you have told us is absolutely the truth. So, now I have to ask both you and Alex a critical question. We have two mini cameras in the car. Would you be willing to try to take some photos of the labs?"

Both men nodded their answer yes.

Then David said, "Do you think you can smuggle the mini cameras in and out of the labs without being caught? And keep in mind the mini cameras are made of plastic. Would they trigger any security systems?"

Alex and Omar looked at each other for a few seconds. Then

Omar said, "I can't be absolutely sure, but I believe the security alarms are designed to respond to metal objects only."

Alex said, "Yes, I agree."

David said, "Let me get the cameras from the car."

He came back with the big, bulky cameras, opened each one, and extracted the mini cameras. Then Helga, who was familiar with these cameras, instructed Alex and Omar in their use. She also made some suggestions on how to best hide the tiny cameras on their bodies. David recommended that they try to obtain photos over the following two weeks, after which they should bring the cameras to Abdul. David then instructed Abdul to place the two mini cameras in a plastic bag and to deposit the bag among the rocks where he had been leaving his messages. Abdul would then have to radio the Mossad that the cameras were ready to be picked up by the MTB.

Finally, David distributed packets of Egyptian currency to Abdul, Alex, and Omar, all of whom showed their gratitude for the funds. As usual, David cautioned them to be very careful and not flash the money around. He also recommended that if the funds were to be deposited in bank accounts, that should be done in small amounts.

With all the business completed, Alex and Omar left one at a time.

Shortly thereafter, David and Helga bid Abdul and his wife good night and drove back to the apartment in Cairo. Once there, Helga made arrangements for their flights back to Israel via Tunis the next day.

9

Aug. 13-23, 1957
Jerusalem, Israel
Mossad Residence

BACK IN JERUSALEM, DAVID AND HELGA GAVE MANNY Epstein a full report on their trip to Egypt, and then knew that they had a number of days to wait for the photos to arrive from Egypt. They spent the time relaxing and enjoying each other's company.

For the first time, they touched on the subject of a future together. David made it very clear that he wanted to marry Helga once their current mission was successfully completed. He also mentioned that if they married, he wanted to transfer out of active field assignments and work instead as an analyst. Helga also felt she wanted to leave field assignments. David asked her if they were to marry, whether she would be willing to relocate to the United States. She thought that over for a while and eventually told David that she would indeed be willing to move to the U.S.

Somehow, the conversations between the two during those days of waiting seemed to create a plan for the future. But all of that had to wait for the end of their current assignment, whenever that might be.

Aug. 24, 1957
Jerusalem, Israel
Mossad Headquarters

THE PHONE CALL from Manny Epstein finally came, asking that the two agents come to the Mossad Headquarters that afternoon. When they arrived, they found both Feingold and Epstein waiting for them.

Feingold said, "Those two mini cameras you left in Egypt have been returned to us. The photos have been processed and analyzed by some of our people, and the results are very disturbing. Based on those photos and our analysis, it appears that this infernal 'Sword of Damocles' project involves two separate and distinct weapons. One is some kind of poison gas, while the other seems to be some tactical nuclear weapons. In any case, both of those weapons could be fatal for Israel. From the photos, it appears that both weapons are possibly some months from being ready for use. Your two contacts at the labs should be able to provide additional information in the coming six to eight weeks. This may mean the two of you may have to go back to Egypt again. We just don't know if and when yet."

David and Helga were silent for some seconds as they mentally digested all this information.

Then David said, "I remember that the point was made that no move could be made against the labs until there was tangible proof that could be shown to the world. I was wondering, do those photos constitute some of that proof?"

Feigned thought about the question and finally said, "Yes, I think these photos could be used as part of the proof we need to show the world. More photos would be extremely helpful. Also, David, do you think that at some future date, those two employees at the labs, Alex and Omar, would be willing to testify? If so,

I suspect we would have to first get them and their families out of Egypt and to safety."

David said, "If Helga and I go back to Egypt, we can check on that as well as request more photos."

Helga said, "Yes, I agree. One more trip might provide answers to additional questions."

Feingold thought this over and then said, "All right, we'll consider what you just said and let you know."

Then Feingold hesitated and seemed to be considering what to say next. Everyone else remained silent, knowing he probably had more to say. Finally, he resumed speaking.

"The Mossad believes it would be dangerous for the two of you to attempt to enter Egypt again by way of commercial flights. You've done it twice already. If the Egyptian authorities realize you are going in and out repeatedly, they may try to arrest you and interrogate you. That could be fatal. So any further trips to Egypt will have to be by MTB. But you should be doubly careful that shore patrols don't get even a whiff of your arriving and departing. So please keep that uppermost in your minds from now on."

With that, the meeting ended, except that Manny Epstein quietly asked the agents if they could come for dinner in two days. David looked at Helga, who simply nodded with a smile, and David said they would be delighted to come.

Aug. 25, 1957
Jerusalem, Israel
The Epstein Residence

When David and Helga arrived at the Epstein home, they received the usual warm reception. During the before-dinner drinks, Manny, with a very serious look on his face, turned to his wife, Esther, and said, "These two criminal types are giving the

Mossad a bad reputation among the world intelligence agencies. They are getting paid and all they do is laze around, go to the beach, and while in Cairo, they went to all the best restaurants. Look at them! They must have put on thirty pounds in the last four months! In the meantime, people like me struggle to make ends meet! I ask you, Esther, does that seem fair?"

David and Helga burst out laughing.

Esther said, "Dear husband, the next time you invite them, I'll make sure they get bread and water and nothing else!"

With that, they all went into the dining room for the usual excellent dinner that Esther always managed to prepare.

During dinner, Esther brought the conversation around to a serious subject.

She looked first at Helga and then at David and asked, "I hope the two of you remember my offer to take care of all the arrangements when you get married. Have you discussed getting married as yet?"

Helga quietly said, "David has told me that he wants to marry me. And yes, I want to marry him. But until this nightmare mission is over and done with, we both feel that we should wait."

Esther said, "Yes, I can see why you want to wait. I only hope and pray that your mission will be over soon!"

And with that, the conversation turned to other happier subjects.

Aug. 27, 1957
Jerusalem, Israel
Mossad Headquarters

A CALL FROM MOSSAD Headquarters alerted David and Helga that their presence was required at Mossad Headquarters. They immediately went there and found Manny Epstein waiting for them. He seemed distracted and tense.

Manny said, “Good morning. I called you here because we had a message from Abdul that the MTB picked up last night. First of all, Abdul said that more film is needed for both of those mini cameras that you gave to Alex and Omar. It sounds as if those two have been taking a lot more photos. Alex and Omar both reported that security seemed to have greatly increased. Finally, the message reported that the actual manufacture of the two weapon systems has started. That may mean that we may have to move against those labs fairly soon. The latest batch of photos is being processed as we speak. Once they are analyzed, there may be another meeting that you two should attend, so try not to be gone from your apartment for any long stretches of time. Any questions?”

Helga asked, “If the MTB deposits more film, do either Alex or Omar know how to load the film into the mini cameras?”

Epstein responded, “That’s an excellent question. When the film is delivered by the MTB, we’ll put a note with the film asking just that.”

On that note, the meeting ended.

Back at their apartment, David and Helga discussed the meaning of what Manny Epstein had just told them.

Helga said, “It sounds to me as if those Nazis might be ready to launch their weapons within 90 to 120 days, maybe. What do you think, David?”

David answered, “Yes, it sure sounds that way. And that’s a pretty scary thought. There’s something else, too. If they are rushing to finish those weapons, they might get careless. That could set off some kind of environmental disaster!”

Helga added, “If you think of how little those Nazis worry about human life, that kind of a disaster is probably the furthest thing from their minds!”

David agreed, and that whole thought made the two agents feel very concerned.

Aug. 29, 1957
Jerusalem, Israel
Massad Headquarters

TWO DAYS LATER, David and Helga were back at Mossad. Headquarters. This time, both Feingold and Epstein were present.

Feingold started the meeting by saying, "We had a short, urgent radio message from Abdul saying that no one there knows how to load the film into those mini cameras and adding that both Alex and Omar were becoming very concerned for their own safety. Also, there have been meetings with the Prime Minister here. He believes the labs will have to be destroyed within six to eight weeks. The military is busy right now trying to decide on how best to accomplish that end result. Helga, we want to send you in via MTB alone to load the film into those mini cameras. We also hope you can meet one last time with Alex and Omar and bring back an updated report that will help the military in their planning."

David exclaimed, "Why is Helga going in alone? We've always gone into Egypt together!"

Feingold immediately answered David. He said, "That's just the point, David. The CIA does not want you to be captured by the SOD. That could cause huge diplomatic problems. But if Helga is caught, it might appear more routine since Israel and Egypt are currently enemies. I'm afraid the decision has already been made. Helga goes in alone!"

David sat there, his mind in turmoil, thinking about the dangers Helga would be facing alone.

Helga said, "David, please remember that I have operated in enemy territory alone in the past. I'll be all right."

David did not know what to say. He sat there feeling more miserable than he had ever felt before in his whole life.

Feingold said in a soothing tone, "Helga is quite correct. She has successfully penetrated Arab countries before. She'll manage just fine."

That evening, as David and Helga lay in bed holding on to each other tightly, David wondered if the best thing that had ever happened to him was now going to be taken away by circumstances.

Aug. 30, 1957
Ashdod, Israel
Israeli Navy Base

In the evening, David drove Helga to Ashdod and the waiting MTB. The drive was silent with both agents tense and upset at being separated. At the dock, David accompanied Helga aboard, where Captain Levy awaited them. Levy sensed the tension in both agents and skipped his usual sardonic comments. Instead, he simply looked at David very directly and said, "David, don't worry. My crew and I will look after Helga as long as she is in our care."

David was so emotionally upset that he could not say a word. He merely took Levy's hand and shook it hard. Then he turned, took Helga in his arms, kissed her, and whispered, "Please come back to me, darling!"

Helga said, "Of course I will, believe it!"

Then David turned and stepped off the MTB. He stood on the dock as the crew cast off and the MTB quietly and slowly slipped out of the harbor. David just stood there watching the sleek MTB disappear in the darkness. He turned to go to the car and suddenly realized tears were streaming down his cheeks. A sense of desperation gripped him as he realized he could lose the person who had become the single most important thing in his life. He got in the car, wiped his tears away, and drove slowly home.

Sept. 1, 1957
Village Near Labs
Abdul's House

A few hours later, the MTB had arrived off the Egyptian coast, and the captain wished Helga good luck just before she climbed down into the inflatable.

Once ashore in Egypt, Helga set off at a brisk but very quiet pace, heading for the village and Abdul's house.

In the early morning hours, she stopped, got off the dirt road, and lay down behind a small hill. There she rested and napped until the sun was well above the horizon. She set off again, and by the time she reached the village, many people were stirring. Soon she arrived at Abdul's small house and was greeted by his wife, Deborah.

Arriving safely there, she heaved a sigh of relief. Helga had to wait until evening before Alex and Omar could show up. She rested and then spent time with Abdul's wife and children.

That evening, after dinner, Alex and Omar arrived separately, both carrying their mini cameras. Helga greeted them and then got busy removing the old cartridges from the mini cameras and replacing them with new ones.

Alex and Omar gave Helga very similar reports. They agreed that the labs were gearing up to begin the manufacture of the two weapon systems: the poison gas and the tactical nuclear cannon shells. They also emphasized that security had indeed become much stricter. Then Alex left, followed fifteen minutes later by Omar.

Helga waited another thirty minutes and then, after bidding Abdul and Deborah goodbye, silently began the hike back to the beach.

As Helga walked along the dirt road in the dark, her thoughts involuntarily strayed to David. She had finally admitted to herself that for the first time since World War II, there was now someone in her life who was truly important. She realized how David, with his kindness, understanding, and protectiveness, had brought her out of the protective shell that she had built for herself after escaping from Treblinka. Now she knew what it meant to be really in love, and she was extremely grateful to David for what he had been able to accomplish for her.

Some hours later, as she approached the seashore, she suddenly heard dogs barking. Helga knew immediately that a security patrol was nearby. She turned and retraced her steps. Walking in the moonlight, she was able to make out a small hill. She got to the backside of the hill and crouched down, her heart beating fast. She hoped the hill would shield her from the security patrol and act as a barrier so that the patrol's dogs would not pick up her scent.

Sure enough, the dogs stopped their barking. Helga listened intently, and it seemed to her that the security patrol was moving off, although she couldn't be sure. She remained hunkered down behind the small hill for a full thirty minutes. Finally, she began slowly and very quietly walking toward the seashore, all her faculties on high alert. But she heard no more dogs barking or guards talking.

Once at the beach, she broadcast the extremely brief message that told the MTB captain that she was ready to be picked up.

Then Helga sat down next to the rocks to wait for the MTB's inflatable to show up. Two and a half hours later, she faintly heard the sound of the inflatable being paddled near the beach. At that moment, she also heard a dog barking not far away. She immediately realized that a patrol had sneaked up on her without her hearing it. Praying that the inflatable would move back offshore, she silently crept around the rocks so as to put them between herself and the dogs of the patrol. She hoped the dogs would lose her scent again if she put the rocks between herself and the patrol.

Evidently, her strategy worked, because after a few more barks the dogs fell silent. Helga waited patiently, knowing she was in very real danger. Concentrating all her hearing, she was barely able to hear the two man patrol with their dogs moving away. She waited a full half hour before sending the MTB another very brief message indicating the crew could try again. Another thirty minutes went by before she thought she heard the inflatable approaching. Just then, she once again heard the barking of dogs and realized that a patrol had approached without her hearing it. This time, she decided that she should not wait for the patrol to pass by. Helga very quietly entered the water and, using a side stroke, managed to put some distance between herself and the shore. Then she managed to dimly see the inflatable not far off.

Reaching the inflatable, Helga scrambled aboard, and the two crewmen began paddling toward the MTB lying a ways offshore. But as the inflatable was a few hundred feet offshore, the three occupants heard dogs barking again. However, the dogs seemed to be some distance away. The crewmen did not stop paddling, and a few minutes later, the barking finally stopped.

Reaching the MTB, Helga was helped aboard, the two crewmen also boarded, the inflatable was pulled on board, and without any further delay, Captain Levy turned the MTB toward Israel. Helga had gone below, and a crewman had wrapped her in a blanket when he realized she was sopping wet and shivering. A few minutes later, the captain joined her below deck. When he saw her condition, he immediately ordered a crewman to heat some soup for her.

Levy said, "Miss Horowitz, I am truly glad to have you back aboard unharmed. I guess that was a close shave for you. By all means, lie down and rest while I get us back to port."

With that, the captain went back on deck, and Helga lay down.

Three hours later, the MTB eased into the harbor and tied up. David was there waiting for Helga. She gave the captain a grateful goodbye, stepped ashore, and was immediately embraced by David. He said not a word, and neither did she. The embrace said it all. They got into their car and left the harbor. The captain had witnessed the embrace and thought to himself, "Thank God I was able to bring her back safely."

Then he, too, left the harbor to return home to his own wife.

Sept. 4, 1957
Jerusalem, Israel
Prime Minister's Conference Room

THAT MORNING, the call came for David and Helga, except that they were to go to the Prime Minister's conference room. That meant an important meeting. When they got there, the room was full of people, including a number of military officers. David saw Feingold, and then he spotted Manny Epstein. Manny waved them over to two empty chairs next to him. Shortly after they sat down, the Prime Minister walked in and everybody stood up. As soon as everyone was seated, the Prime Minister began speaking.

"You have all been called here today because events are moving rather quickly. Thanks to Miss Horowitz sitting over there, we now have more definitive information regarding this 'Sword of Damocles' project that Nasser and those Nazis have cooked up. Miss Horowitz, we are all indebted to you for bringing back that information. And, incidentally, I was delighted and relieved that you made it back safely. The MTB captain passed on to my office news of the narrow escape you had. If Egyptian security had caught you, it would have been bad enough, but if you had fallen into the hands of that butcher, Rochman, we might well have never seen you ever again. So congratulations on coming back to us safe and sound."

At that, everyone applauded. Helga merely smiled and nodded her thanks.

Ben Gurion continued, "Based on this latest information, it seems that Israel must move against the 'Sword of Damocles' no later than four weeks from now. We have sufficient photographic evidence to prove to the world that this entire project was designed to destroy Israel. If some countries want to condemn us, so be it. But we must defend ourselves."

Ben Gurion stopped talking for a few seconds to organize his thoughts, then continued.

"I have been in touch with President Eisenhower in Washington, who agreed completely that we now have no choice but to act to destroy the 'Sword' project. He suggested that when the time is right, he could deploy a portion of the U.S. 6th Fleet to international waters off the northern coast of Egypt. These naval units will not take part in our military operation. Instead, they will be carrying out a training exercise that will involve round-the-clock carrier operations. This should distract the Egyptian radar and their military and make it easier for us to land a strike force in Egypt near the labs. I have already given orders to the Israeli Defense Force to begin the necessary planning immediately."

Again, Ben Gurion stopped, then picked up the narrative again.

"The Knesset has been briefed on the situation, and there was unanimous consent for our intervention, even by the Arab members. You will all be kept advised as the planning is carried out. I don't think that I need to stress the absolute necessity for the utmost secrecy about all of this. Do not discuss it at home or anywhere else. Thank you all for coming today, and we shall meet again in the near future."

With that, the Prime Minister stood up, as did everyone else, and he walked out. The room was silent as everyone digested what they had just heard. People began filtering out of the conference room.

Manny Epstein leaned over and said, "Helga and David, please meet me in my office."

David and Helga drove to the Mossad Headquarters and caught up with Manny Epstein in his office. He immediately said to Helga, "When I told Esther how you almost got caught by that beach patrol with the dogs, she became truly upset. I had to calm her down. But that's not the reason I asked you here. We received a message from Abdul saying that he, Alex, Omar, and their families are all seeking asylum in Israel. I'm pretty sure they all understand that they can't leave Egypt right now without creating suspicion on the part of the Nazis and others. I'm also pretty sure the right time to extricate them from Egypt will be when the IDF attacks. I will coordinate with those who are planning that mission. Then those three families will have to be informed at the last moment on what to do. I've already cleared all of this with Feingold, and he agreed. He feels, as I do, that those three men have risked everything in order to help us, and granting them asylum is the least we can do in return."

David and Helga agreed completely with that and then went back to their Mossad residence.

Sept. 5, 1957
Jerusalem, Israel
Mossad Headquarters

The following day, David and Helga were asked to come to the Mossad Headquarters and meet with both Feingold and Epstein. When they arrived there, they found one additional participant, a full Colonel from the Israeli Defense Force (IDF). He was introduced as Colonel Abraham Levin. Levin spoke perfect English and appeared to be young for his rank.

Feingold chaired the meeting and immediately began speaking.

He said, "Colonel Levin is in charge of putting together the plan for the destruction of the 'Sword of Damocles' project. So Colonel, why don't you lead off?"

Levin cleared his throat and began speaking.

He said, "Mr. Knox and Miss Horowitz, you were invited to this meeting because of your past involvement with this 'Sword' project. We at the IDF see the attack on the 'Sword' to have a number of goals. These are: 1) the destruction of the labs, 2) the capture of the three Nazi Colonels, 3) the removal of small amounts of both the poison gas and of one of the tactical nuclear shells, 4) the safe evacuation of all those workers, and 5) the safe transfer to Israel of those three Egyptians and their families who helped us by supplying critically important information. This plan of attack will include the fact that a Task Group of the U.S. 6th Fleet will be operating not very far from where the IDF will mount its attack. Basically, that is the picture as the IDF sees it right now."

Total silence followed the Colonel's view of what was involved in the coming operation. Everyone was looking down at the table, trying to understand what would be needed to carry out the complex operation successfully. Finally, David hesitatingly raised his hand to be recognized. Feingold said, "Go ahead, David."

David plunged in and said, "Regarding the saving of those who helped us, I think Helga and I may be in the best position to figure out a successful strategy for getting them out of Egypt safely. As regards the actual attack, it seems to me the best approach might be a two-prong attack. A paratroop drop could seal off the labs, while a shore landing not far from the labs would involve the main force. But I don't know if any of that makes any sense to you, Colonel Levin?"

Levin responded in a tone of admiration, "Mr. Knox, your

approach might be just what is needed. I will bring it back to our planning people, and let's see how they feel about it."

Feingold said, "Colonel, that certainly seems to be an approach worth serious consideration. Tell me, Colonel, when do you think we all should meet again with some response from the IDF?"

Levin thought for a few seconds and then said, "I think that if I built a fire under the planning group, I may have an initial reaction within a week."

Feingold said, "Fine, let's tentatively plan on meeting here in a week. You'll all be advised as to what time."

That ended the meeting. On the way home, Helga said in an admiring tone, "David, your suggestions were brilliant!"

David just shrugged and said modestly, "It was just what made sense to me. But we'll have to see if the IDF agrees."

Sept. 6-12, 1957
Jerusalem, Israel
Mossad Residence

KNOWING THAT THERE would be little for them to do for a week, David and Helga spent much of that time relaxing, going to the beach, and at times discussing their possible future together. A call did come from Esther Epstein inviting them to dinner, which they accepted gladly.

Sept. 13, 1957
Jerusalem, Israel
The Epstein Residence

AS USUAL, WHEN David and Helga reached the Epstein home, Esther greeted them with hugs. More and more, the Epsteins were treating David and Helga as if they were their own children, and the two responded gratefully to the obvious affection and esteem that the Epsteins displayed. Over dinner, Manny gently broached a subject that David and Helga had pretty much avoided.

Manny asked, “Have you two love birds given any more thought to your future after this ‘Sword of Damocles’ insanity is destroyed?”

David looked at Helga but said nothing. Finally, Helga broke the silence.

She said, “David and I are very much in love, and if we get through this operation safely, we want to get married. Beyond that, and speaking for myself only, I don’t think I want to continue with field operations. I’ve had enough excitement!”

David chimed in, “I have to agree with Helga. I, too, want to get married, and I am ready to ask the CIA for an office job. No more field work!”

Manny smiled in a fatherly way and said, “I have to agree with the two of you. You both have had enough excitement to last a lifetime. But Helga, how would you feel about living in the United States?”

Helga answered, “If David goes back to America, I want to go with him.”

With that, it seemed as if David and Helga had pretty much made up their minds.

Esther said, “You two don’t forget, before you run off to America, that I want to make a beautiful wedding for you!”

Helga said, “Esther, how could David and I possibly forget such a fantastic offer. I just don’t know how we could ever repay you?”

Manny said, “That’s easy. Once you settle down somewhere in the U.S., Esther and I will have an excuse to travel to America so as to visit you! It’s about time Esther and I did some traveling for fun. After all, we’re not getting any younger, you know!”

David and Helga had happy expressions on their faces at the thought of future visits from the Epsteins.

On the way home, Helga suddenly said to David, "You know we are truly lucky to have friends like Manny and Esther!"

David could only agree wholeheartedly.

Sept. 14, 1957
Jerusalem, Israel
Prime Minister's Conference Room

WHEN DAVID AND HELGA arrived at the Prime Minister's conference room, they found the room full of people, most of whom they did not recognize. Feingold and Epstein were there, as well as Colonel Levin. Shortly thereafter, the meeting began and was chaired by a civilian who obviously represented the Prime Minister. He introduced everyone there and then turned to Colonel Levin and asked the Colonel what the status of the planning was for the attack and destruction of the 'Sword of Damocles.'

Colonel Levin responded, "The planning is underway, but is not yet complete. We have been in touch with the Admiral in command of the U.S. 6th Fleet so that there will not be any confusion between us on the day we raid the labs."

Here Levin stopped for a few seconds, then, looking directly at David, continued.

He said, "Mr. Knox, it turns out that our planners were thinking pretty much along the same lines as you mentioned at the last meeting. It looks as if both you and Miss Horowitz may be asked to participate in the raid in some way. Congratulations on your thoughts regarding the raid."

David looked down at the conference table and remained silent.

Colonel Levin continued, "One of the items that has come up during the planning is how we should deal with the people working at the labs as well as the construction crews working on the above-ground structure. For both political and humanitarian reasons, we would try to find a way to spare the lives of those workers who really don't know anything about the 'Sword of Damocles' plot. To accomplish that goal, we need some additional information. So, Mr. Knox and Miss Horowitz, we are wondering whether you two would be willing to volunteer to go back into Egypt one more time before the attack and try to obtain the information we are seeking. If you do volunteer, then you would be briefed on what exactly we hope to find out."

The Colonel stopped his briefing and looked at David and Helga. David, in turn, learned over to Helga and very quietly asked, "What do you think?"

Helga thought for a few moments and then softly said, "I guess we really should do this one more time."

David looked at Levin and said, "Colonel, we'll go in one last time."

Levin said in an admiring tone, "Good for you!"

At that point, the room exploded into spontaneous applause as everyone there clearly understood the danger David and Helga would be facing.

Levin then said, "If you, Mr. Knox and Miss Horowitz, will come to this conference room tomorrow at 9, you'll be briefed."

The meeting continued for some time, but with no definitive plan of action from the IDF, it finally ended with everyone present waiting for a future meeting and a definite plan.

On the way back to the Mossad Residence, David and Helga discussed their forthcoming and hopefully last incursion into enemy territory.

David said, "I sure hope we didn't make a big mistake volunteering to go in one more time. It just seemed the right thing to do."

Helga said, "I agree. We'll just have to be doubly careful this time!"

David answered, "Amen to that!"

And with that, nothing more was said that day as the two waited for the briefing to come the next day.

Sept. 15, 1957
Jerusalem, Israel
Prime Minister's Conference Room

WHEN DAVID AND HELGA arrived the following morning, they found only Manny Epstein and Colonel Levin in the room.

Levin thanked them for coming and immediately began their briefing.

He said, "We at the IDF believe the attack should come on a morning when the labs are functioning normally. That would give us the best chance of capturing the three Nazi Colonels before they have any inkling as to what is happening. Unfortunately, that means attacking in broad daylight, not a great idea!"

David interrupted, "Colonel, what if a portion of the attack force is landed during the night. Then, if we can tell you at what time all the workers are present, that would be the time to make the paratroop drop, which could seal off the building. At the same time, the troops that had been landed on shore would move forward and join the paratroops."

Levin said, "Hmm, that might just work well. I'll suggest that approach. Now, we need Alex and Omar to be absent from the labs and ready to be evacuated along with Abdul and all their families. They probably need to drive at night to the shore location where we are going to land troops. One or two of the landing barges that bring in troops can then take the three families out and bring them to Israel. We're not sure yet as to how best to coordinate the evacuation of these three families."

Here Levin paused, unsure of how to continue.

David once again spoke up.

He said, "Colonel, if I may, it seems to me that when Miss Horowitz and I go to Egypt this next time to get the additional information that is needed, we can also coordinate with the three families that have to be evacuated. At the same time, we can find out the normal work schedule of the labs and maybe get a layout of the entire building, which might make things simpler for the troops when they have to enter the building."

Colonel Levin agreed that having the two agents make one more trip into Egypt was worth the risk of their being discovered by a patrol or by security forces.

Manny Epstein, who had been silent up to now, spoke up.

Epstein said, "David, do you and Helga really want to go back in one more time? It seems to be a potential gamble to me."

David looked at Helga and then responded, "I think I can speak for Helga as well as myself. Sure, it's a gamble. But we have been involved so far, and I think we both want to see this whole operation through to the end."

Colonel Levin asked, "Mr. Knox, how soon could you and Miss Horowitz be ready to enter Egypt again?"

David responded, "I'd say as soon as the Mossad can set it up."

Manny Epstein said, "I think we can easily arrange for the specially equipped MTB to be ready by tomorrow night."

David looked at Helga with raised eyebrows as if to ask what she thought. Helga merely nodded her agreement.

David said, "Colonel, we can go in tomorrow night and be back two or three days later, depending on how quickly Alex and Omar can be contacted and how soon they can come to Abdul's house with the necessary information."

Colonel Levin nodded and said, "O.K. then. As soon as you two agents are back and we can process your information, then we at the IDF should be able to complete our plans for the attack on the labs. Mr. Knox and Miss Horowitz, I personally want to express my thanks and my admiration for what you have already accomplished and for going in harm's way again."

Colonel Levin left the room, but Manny Epstein signaled the two agents to remain.

He said, "I want you two to know that the Mossad is truly grateful for your willingness to enter Egypt one more time. And after you get back, Esther has already commanded me to tell you that she wants you over for dinner, if you are available."

Helga said, "For one of Esther's dinners, I'm willing to spit in President Nasser's face!"

Everyone laughed at that remark.

On that note, the meeting ended and David and Helga went back to their apartment to wait for the following night and their trip once more on the MTB.

Sept. 16, 1957
Ashdod Harbor, Israel
Israeli Naval Base

THAT EVENING, David and Helga boarded the same MTB and kidded around with the captain, whom by now they had gotten to know fairly well. Then they went below to rest as the crew got the MTB underway.

Captain Levy came below and, feigning anger, said, "Look, you two, I'm going to start charging big fees for all this running back and forth to Egypt. My wife just refuses to believe me when I tell her that I'm on nighttime missions. She is absolutely convinced that I'm seeing another woman. Now, you tell me, how do I get out of this jam? You two are ruining my marriage!"

Helga said, "Tell her you are having a secret affair with one of President Nasser's girlfriends and that's why you have to run over to Egypt so often!"

Levy laughed and said, "I'll try telling her that, but I've got a feeling she won't believe me!"

Some time later, the captain came below and told them it was almost time to get aboard the inflatable.

The usual two crewmen paddled them toward shore until suddenly the silence of the night was abruptly interrupted by the loud barking of two dogs. Without another word, the two crewmen turned the inflatable around and paddled further offshore. Then they stopped paddling and waited to see what would happen next.

After a couple of minutes, the dogs stopped barking as they evidently lost the scent. Nevertheless, the crewmen waited for thirty minutes before once again silently approaching the beach. Once there, the two agents lost no time scrambling ashore as the inflatable disappeared in the night.

This time, David and Helga were more careful than ever before as they hiked silently toward the distant village where Abdul and his family lived.

Sunrise found them lying behind the small hill that overlooked the village. Since no one was stirring in the village at that early hour, they made the impromptu decision to walk quickly to Abdul's house and hide in the shed he had on his small property. They waited there until 9 in the morning before moving to the house and knocking on the door.

Abdul himself welcomed them with a broad smile, followed by his wife. They had been warned by a coded message of the impending visit by David and Helga, whom by now they looked on as trusted friends. As usual, Abdul's wife fed them breakfast. Then Abdul told them that Alex and Omar were not sure when they would be able to meet with them. David asked Abdul if it would be possible for him to ask Alex to bring a layout of the entire building. Abdul said he would try to pass the request to

Alex or his wife. Then the two agents retreated to the shed to rest and await the arrival of Alex and Omar.

Sept. 18, 1957
Village Near Labs
Abdul's House

Two full days elapsed before Alex and Omar had an opportunity to visit Abdul's house in circumstances they felt were reasonably safe. During that time, David and Helga had to wait patiently. They spent part of the time with Abdul's wife and children.

Finally, on the evening of the 18th, after dark, Alex and Omar arrived separately. There were warm greetings all around, and Alex gave David a set of small blueprints of the underground labs as well as of the fake hosiery mill built above them at ground level. The blueprints were protected in a plastic bag that was sealed. David thanked him and then began his briefing.

David said, "I can tell you that soon there will be an attack on the building where you work by the Israeli Defense Force. You will be given the day and time a few hours before it actually starts. It has been decided that you three and your entire families are to be evacuated to Israel a short time before the attack actually begins."

"You and your families will have to hike to the beach at night, and it will be absolutely essential that no patrol discovers you. It is possible that Helga and I will come back here and lead you to the appropriate spot on the beach. I'm really not sure yet. The Israeli Navy will then evacuate all of you."

David paused to collect his thoughts, then continued.

"You will have to leave all your belongings behind. You can take only money and jewelry with you. If you think it is safe, you can take most of any money that you have in bank accounts out, but leave a small amount so as not to make anyone at the bank suspicious. Make up some fictitious stories as to why you need to take those funds out."

David paused again to make sure he wasn't forgetting something, then went on with his briefing.

"You will not have much warning as to when you have to leave for the beach. I'll try to get two very short messages to Abdul. The first will be your signal to get ready, including getting funds out of any bank accounts you may have. A few days later, Abdul, you will get a second message that will give you about twelve hours' advance warning to move to the beach that night. Alex and Omar, in order for you to know about the two messages that I will send to Abdul, I think your wives will have to start visiting Abdul's grocery store every day after the first message arrives. I don't know of any other safe way to do this."

David stopped talking, then turned to Helga and asked, "Helga, what else do they need to know?"

Helga said, "You and your wives need to know that as soon as you reach Israel, there is an organization that will take care of all your needs. You will be provided with temporary housing, meals, and any medical attention you may need. I strongly recommend you wait to tell your children anything until the last possible moment. You also have to be careful about giving the people you report to at the labs any inkling that you'll be leaving. Lastly, you all have to be very quiet when you leave your homes and hike to the beach. Your children must absolutely understand this. I recommend that on the evening of the evacuation, all three families gather here at Abdul's house and have an evening meal. If it is possible, David and I will meet you here later that night."

Helga paused and looked at David to see what else needed to be said.

David asked, "At what time does the workday begin at the labs, and are the three Nazi Colonels there by that time?"

Omar answered, "We begin working at 7:30, and the Nazis are always there then or by 8 at the latest. Also, we work Sunday through Thursday and get Friday and Saturday off."

David asked, "Do you have any questions?"

No one seemed to have any. Alex and Omar thanked David and Helga profusely. First, Alex and, some time later, Omar left to go back home.

David and Helga were left alone with Abdul and his wife.

Helga commented, "I sure hope Alex and Omar don't do anything to arouse suspicion!"

David chimed in, "Amen!"

Abdul said, "You should keep in mind that we are living in a dictatorship here in Egypt. So as a result, we all learn at an early age to keep our mouths shut and to not show our true feelings."

David looked at Helga and said, "I guess we did what we came for, and it's time to get back to the beach and the MTB."

Helga agreed and said, "I guess so. Abdul, can you please send a signal to the MTB that we should be back at the beach no later than four hours from now?"

Abdul said, "Yes, of course, I'll do it immediately!"

Sept. 18, 1957
North of Cairo, Egypt
Area Near Labs

TWENTY MINUTES LATER, the two agents quietly slipped out of Abdul's house and set off for the beach.

As always, they walked quietly and without speaking, listening for any signs of patrols. Three hours later, as they approached the beach, they suddenly heard the barking of dogs. Helga grabbed David's arm and turned to go back the way they had come. They retreated about a quarter of a mile, at which point the barking stopped.

David and Helga waited another fifteen minutes, then set off for the beach once more. As soon as they reached the beach, David flashed the light signal that he sincerely hoped the MTB crew would see.

As David and Helga approached the beach, the dogs began barking again. Helga grabbed David's hand and whispered, "We've got to get into the water!"

She pulled David with her and walked into the cold Mediterranean. She and David continued walking forward until the water was up to their necks. At that point, the dogs stopped barking as they lost the scent once more.

The two agents remained standing in the cold water without moving for some time. Eventually, they could dimly make out the outline of the approaching inflatable.

Helga called out in a soft tone, "Over here, we're over here!"

The crewmen paddling the inflatable heard her call and steered in their direction. The agents had difficulty pulling themselves aboard the inflatable due to the weight of their waterlogged clothing and the weight of their backpacks. The two crewmen finally pulled them aboard and began paddling quietly toward the invisible MTB lying some distance away.

Suddenly, the night's silence was ripped apart by the sound of three gunshots. One of the guards of the security patrol thought he could see something in the water and decided to take action.

Helga, sitting next to David, suddenly heard him gasp and then groan loudly. She turned and whispered, "David, what's wrong?"

David, in great pain, managed to whisper back, "I've been shot!"

Helga, without knowing where David had been shot, said to

the crewmen, "Quick! Row as hard as you can! I've got to get this man aboard the MTB! He's been shot!"

The crewmen understood the urgency of the moment and began paddling as hard as they could. In short order, they reached the MTB, and Captain Levy, who had heard the shots, leaned over the side and asked, "Anyone hurt?"

Helga, now on the verge of panic, said, "David's been hit, I don't know how badly!"

Captain Levy lost no time in taking control of the emergency. He called for two additional crewmen to assist in getting David aboard and below decks. There, Captain Levy took one look at David's wound and immediately began barking orders.

He called out, "Bring me the medical kit here! Also, get me hot water, bandages, and blankets!"

David, by this time, was semi-comatose and obviously in great pain. Captain Levy ordered Helga, who was standing nearby, "Help me take his upper clothes off! He's been hit in the upper chest and he's bleeding badly!"

Levy and Helga managed to get David's shirt and undershirt off, both blood-soaked, and the captain immediately applied a pressure bandage to try to staunch the bleeding. Then he gave David an injection of morphine to reduce the pain and finally covered David with two blankets. David was trembling, and it was obvious that he was on the verge of going into shock.

Then Levy said to Helga, "I've got to get us back to Ashdod as quickly as possible. He's in bad shape! Stay with him and yell if you see any change in his condition!"

With that, Captain Levy rushed back to the bridge and gave orders to get the MTB moving as fast as possible. The crew rapidly complied, and within two minutes, the MTB was rushing through the night at close to 30 knots, which caused the entire boat to vibrate. Levy came back below decks, checked on David, and then told Helga to get undressed so he could get her wet outer clothes dried out in the hot engine room. He also told Helga to get under the blankets next to David and help keep him warm with her own body heat. She quickly did as Levy had ordered.

During the next two and a half hours, the MTB rushed through the night toward Ashdod. The crew was very quiet, realizing the urgency and seriousness of the situation.

Eventually, the MTB reached Ashdod Harbor, where an ambulance was already waiting. David was quickly but gently taken off the MTB on a stretcher and placed in the ambulance, where the nurses immediately started a blood transfusion and an IV.

As Helga was getting off the MTB, Captain Levy stopped her for a few seconds and said, "Good luck and God Bless!" With that, he gave Helga a brief hug and then turned away, not wanting to reveal his own emotional concern for David. Helga raced to her car, and as the ambulance left the harbor, she followed it to the Beth Israel Hospital in Tel Aviv, a very large facility well able to care for trauma victims such as David.

The hospital had been forewarned that a gunshot victim was on the way, and as soon as the ambulance arrived, David was rushed to an operating room, where a surgical team, already scrubbed, was waiting.

When Helga entered the hospital, a female employee met her and took her to a waiting room. The employee got some hot soup for Helga and showed her how she could be reached. Then she left Helga to herself and her terrifying thoughts about David.

Ninety minutes later, as Helga was sitting on a love seat with her eyes closed, she felt someone sitting down next to her. She opened her eyes to see Esther Epstein there with Manny nearby. Helga was unable to say anything. She simply began sobbing on Esther's shoulder, who in turn held her tightly.

Another hour passed by with very little conversation among the three visitors. Finally, a middle-aged man in green scrub clothes appeared. He evidently knew who to look for because he came directly up to Helga and said, “Miss Horowitz, I’m Doctor Abrams. We just finished operating on Mr. Knox. If he had gotten here an hour or two later, I don’t think we could have saved him. Mr. Knox lost a great deal of blood and was going into shock when we got him into the operating room.”

“The bullet penetrated his chest very close to his heart. A quarter of an inch to the right, and that bullet would have struck a corner of his heart, and he would have died very quickly. So he was actually very lucky. He is alive, but he has to get through the next twenty-four hours. If he makes it, he should recover without any problems since he’s young and fit. He is in Intensive Care, and we are letting him sleep. As for you, Miss Horowitz, I strongly advise that you go home and get some rest. We will call you tomorrow with an update on his condition. Now go home!”

Helga just stood there, not sure what to say, but Esther Epstein, standing next to her, said, “Thank you, Doctor Abrams. I’ll make sure Miss Horowitz goes home!”

Dr. Abrams nodded and left. Esther said, “Helga, Manny is going to drive your car, and you are coming with me, and we are going to get you home!”

And that was precisely what they did. When the Epsteins got Helga to the government building where she and David lived, they first took her to the communal dining room and made sure she ate a large breakfast. Then they took her to her and David’s apartment and saw to it that she lay down and got some sleep. Esther said she was going to stay with Helga until the next day, and Helga was too tired and distraught to argue with Esther.

That same morning, Colonel Rochman, back in the labs, had been informed of the nighttime incident at the beach and of one of the beach patrol guards firing three shots at what he thought might have been something floating near the beach. When Rochman asked for more information, he was advised that there was no more information to be had. Hearing this, he flew into a rage and threatened to have both members of the beach patrol summarily executed. Eventually, he calmed down enough to rescind the execution order.

Sept. 19, 1957
Tel Aviv, Israel
Beth Israel Hospital

THE NEXT MORNING, the hospital called and told Helga that she could visit David for a few minutes. Esther drove Helga to the hospital. There, Helga spent five minutes visiting David. He was obviously in bad shape, but according to the staff, he was recovering very nicely. In fact, later that day, David was moved to a private patient room, and Helga was informed that the following day she could come and sit with him all day, which she did.

Sept. 20, 1957
Tel Aviv, Israel
Beth Israel Hospital

HELGA WAS SITTING in the private patient room assigned to David, reading and keeping a close eye on David, who was napping on and off because of his greatly weakened condition. The door to the room suddenly and quietly opened, and Helga looked up to see Captain Erik Levy, the MTB captain, peek in. When Levy determined it was all right to enter, he did so and came to stand near David's bed. David opened his eyes and whispered, "Hello, Captain."

Levy put on a fake angry look and said, "Don't try to be nice. I'm mad as hell at both of you! You two miserable clowns are giving me, my crew, and my MTB a bad reputation. I'm going to ask the big shots to get someone else to haul you guys back and forth to Egypt. And furthermore, you got blood all over the upper deck and below decks, too. You two sure are real trouble makers!"

David smiled weakly, and Helga giggled.

Then the captain went on to say, "David, you really look like shit! And Helga, you don't look much better!"

That produced more smiles and giggles.

Then Levy said, "And I want you guys to know that my wife gave me plain and fancy hell for coming home with blood all over my nice clean uniform! She thinks I was in a fight! Can you believe that?"

Then Levy turned serious and said, "I was just told that you are going to make a complete recovery. That's great! When we first got you aboard, I was really wondering if we'd get you back to Ashdod and real medical care in time. You might be interested to know that we set some kind of speed record getting back to Ashdod. We were doing over thirty knots all the way, and the engines were beginning to overheat. It's a good thing the engine mechanics kept my engines in great shape!"

Helga got up and embraced Levy. Then she said, "Captain, David and I will never be able to thank you enough for saving his life!"

Levy answered, "It's all part of the job. But what do I tell my wife about all these night trips? She still believes I am out with another woman! I tell you, this job can really ruin a marriage! Anyhow, David, get well soon. And Helga, take care of this idiot you seem to care for so much!"

With a wave and a broad smile, Captain Levy walked out of the room.

Helga, speaking softly, said, "What a wonderful person he is!"

David looked at her and simply nodded his head.

Sept. 20-30, 1957
Tel Aviv & Jerusalem, Israel
Beth Israel Hospital & Mossad Residence

OVER THE NEXT TEN DAYS, David made an amazingly fast recovery. After only five more days in the hospital, he was discharged and told to go home to finish his convalescence. Under the watchful eye of Helga, he got stronger each day and, once back in the Mossad apartment, he went for long walks together with Helga. His chest wound healed nicely, and the stitches were removed.

In the meantime, Helga had submitted a report to Mossad Headquarters about their last trip to the village.

Then a phone call came from Esther Epstein asking whether David was up to coming over for dinner. The answer Esther received was an enthusiastic "YES."

Oct 1, 1957
Jerusalem, Israel
The Epstein Residence

A FEW DAYS AFTER David was considered to be totally recovered, Helga got a phone call requesting their presence the following day at the Prime Minister's conference room. This was followed a couple of hours later by a call from Manny Epstein asking whether David and Helga could come to the Epsteins' for one of Esther's dinners. David had taken the call, and as Manny asked if they could come over that evening, David winked at Helga sitting nearby and answered, "Hold on, Manny, let me check with my executive secretary and see if our presence is required either in Washington or Hollywood or maybe in Cairo."

That brought loud laughter from Manny over the phone.

Helga grabbed the phone from David and said, "Manny, we'll be delighted to come for dinner. Thank you very much!"

Manny answered, "See you around 7. And tell that wise guy you live with that if he is otherwise occupied, we'll be happy to have just have you come over!"

And without waiting for a response, Manny hung up. Helga relayed the message to David, and the two had a good laugh.

That evening, the two agents arrived right on time, and both got bear hugs from Esther. Manny was there too, home from the office. They all sat down for drinks, and Esther, with a very serious look, said, "I understand you had a close shave when leaving Egypt this time!"

David said, "Thank God Helga is a quick thinker. It was her idea to get into the water all the way up to our necks. That prevented those patrol dogs from smelling our scent."

Helga just smiled while David, sitting beside her on a love seat, took her hand.

Esther remarked, "See, David, women are good for something more than just making babies and cooking!"

This brought a laugh from all four occupants.

Then Esther asked in her usual direct manner, "David, are you really completely recovered from your gunshot wound?"

David answered, "Yes, Esther, I'm pretty much recovered. My only problem is that I still lack some of my usual energy, but I'm getting better every day, I'm happy to say!"

Esther smiled at that and said no more about the entire incident.

Later, sitting around the dinner table, Esther brought the conversation around to the topic of their future.

Esther asked, "Have you two talked about your future after this 'Sword of Damocles' nightmare is over?"

Helga looked at David and then turned to Esther. She said, "No, we haven't really talked about that much. I think we both have been putting it off until after this mission is over. I also think that I have had enough field work. I love David very much, and assuming we get married, I would not mind living in America. But I can't speak for David."

David said, "I agree with Helga. I too want to leave field work. Maybe I can work for the CIA as an analyst. And I most definitely want to marry Helga. But not before we are done with this mission."

Manny, who had been silent until now, broke in and said, "I agree totally that any marriage plans should wait until the current mission is over and done with. Now, Esther, if David and Helga settle down in America, that would give us an excuse to visit the U.S. once or twice a year!"

That brought laughs all around.

Esther said, "I hope you haven't forgotten my invitation to make your wedding for you. I don't think you have any idea how happy that would make Manny and me!"

Helga said, "No, we haven't forgotten. I think once the mission is finished, we can sit down and talk about it."

David agreed.

On that happy note, the evening ended.

Oct. 2, 1957
Jerusalem, Israel
Prime Minister's Conference Room

THAT MORNING, David and Helga headed for the Prime Minister's offices. When they entered the Prime Minister's conference room, they found it packed with a great many more people than at any prior time. Feigned and Epstein were there, as was Colonel Levin from the IDF.

The Prime Minister was not there, but a man who identified himself as Isaac Perlman and was the Prime Minister's Chief of

Staff ran the meeting. A rather large number of IDF officers in uniform were present. David and Helga found seats against one wall and waited patiently for the meeting to begin. Eventually, Perlman stood, introduced himself, and then asked Colonel Levin to bring everyone up to date.

Levin stood up and began his briefing.

Levin said, "The IDF has set a date for the attack and destruction of the labs in Egypt. Thanks to the Mossad, specifically Mr. Knox and Miss Horowitz, we know we have blueprints of the labs and the fake mill above it. These will help greatly, so thanks to you both."

Levin stopped and pointed to David and Helga, and as a result, there was a round of applause.

Levin continued, "The IDF will land a brigade of 2,000 members on the beach at a point nearest to the labs at approximately 7 a.m. on D-Day. That force will wait until after 8 a.m., when the labs begin their workday, to move toward the labs. We have arranged that at 8 a.m., the U.S. 6th Fleet operating in the Western Mediterranean will begin a training exercise that will involve carrier aircraft operating about twenty miles north of Alexandria over open water and well clear of the Egyptian territorial borders. We hope this will distract the Egyptian radar operators as well as keep any Egyptian fighters on the ground."

"A portion of the attack force, around 200 troops, will be dropped by parachute very close to the labs around 9:30 a.m. and will encircle the building, completely cutting off any possibility of escape."

Levin paused, took a sip of coffee, and then continued.

"Based on our current information, we plan to let all the employees have their freedom with the exception of the three Nazi Colonels who are to be brought back to Israel for trial. It is possible that a few of the higher-level management people may be detained for questioning. We are going to attempt to remove all of the poison gas containers and bring those back to Israel. With the nuclear material, it is a different story. We will remove a small amount together with one shell casing as proof of what was being planned."

Levin paused once more, drank more coffee, then resumed his briefing.

"When all of that is accomplished and everyone has been evacuated from the building, a demolition team will move in. Explosive charges will be distributed throughout the building, which will be remotely triggered. Once the demolition team has moved a safe distance away, the charges will be set off. In the meantime, the majority of the attack force will be moving at their best speed toward the pickup point for evacuation. And that, ladies and gentlemen, is the basic attack plan. Are there any questions or comments?"

Perlman stood and thanked Colonel Levin and then asked a couple of pertinent questions.

He said, "Colonel, does the IDF expect any casualties as a result of this attack?"

Colonel Levin replied, "No, sir, we believe the surprise will be so great and the whole operation of such short duration that we should not expect any casualties!"

Then Perlman asked, "What if the Egyptian Air Force attempts to interfere?"

Levin answered, "Fighter aircraft of the IDF will be ready for take-off and will engage if Egyptian aircraft are launched."

Then Perlman said, "As you know, Colonel, the Prime Minister is very anxious to locate the three Nazi Colonels, bring them back to Israel, and prosecute them. Do you think you'll have any difficulty identifying them?"

Levin responded, "We hope not. However, we know that Miss Horowitz, an agent of the Mossad, would easily recognize Colonel Rochman, one of the Nazis. For that reason, the IDF would greatly appreciate it if she were part of the brigade that assaults the labs."

Perlman, who knew what Helga looked like, turned to her and asked, "Miss Horowitz, would you be willing to go into the labs with the assault force?"

Helga glanced at David and then answered, "Yes, sir, I'm willing to do that. But rather than land on the beach with the assault force, I think it would be better if I could land either many hours earlier or, better yet, the night before. That would give me a chance to alert the three families that hope to be evacuated and help them get to the rendezvous point at the beach."

David could not restrain himself and blurted out, "Colonel, you know who I am. I want to go along with Miss Horowitz!"

Before Levin could respond, Finegold broke in. He had sat silent until now, but felt he should speak up.

Finegold said, "Miss Horowitz and Mr. Knox have entered Egypt successfully a number of times. It seems to me that inserting them twenty-four hours before the assault makes sense. Together, they can alert the three families the day before the assault, bring them to the beach the night before the assault, and then they could enter the labs as part of the assault force."

"However, we need to remember that the last time Miss Horowitz and Mr. Knox were inserted into Egypt via an MTB, they almost got caught coming out. In fact, Mr. Knox came close to losing his life when he was shot by a shore patrol guard as the two of them were being transported to the MTB in order to be extricated from Egypt."

Levin thought about this for a bit and finally nodded.

He said, "Yes, if these two agents are willing to face the risks involved, it would probably work to everybody's advantage to follow that plan."

Perlman said, "Miss Horowitz and Mr. Knox, are you both

willing to go in one last time? If so, you will be inserted into Egypt about twenty-four hours before the attack."

David and Helga looked at each other but said nothing. Finally, Helga spoke up and said, "Yes, sir, Mr. Perlman, we are in agreement!"

Perlman said, "Thank you both for your participation and courage. Mr. Feingold, you'll see to it that the arrangements will be made for both the insertion and extraction of these agents plus the evacuation of the three families."

Feingold answered, "Yes, absolutely, the Mossad will take care of all of that."

The meeting continued for some time as various details of the attack were discussed, although these had little to do with the participation of David and Helga. Eventually, the meeting ended, and the two agents made their way home. In the afternoon, Helga suggested they go for a long walk throughout Jerusalem, and David agreed. The two agents walked for a long time, hand in hand, saying little. The forthcoming military operation and their part in it loomed over them like a nightmare. After their walk, David suggested they eat dinner at a small restaurant they both liked. Dinner was good, but very quiet.

After dinner, they retired to their apartment, took showers, and got ready for bed. But once they got into bed, by mutual unspoken consent, they made love in a way that seemed desperate. Afterwards, as they lay in an embrace, Helga spoke what was on both their minds.

She said, "David, I love you very much and I don't want to lose you. I think this should be the last field assignment for both of us."

David immediately agreed and said he felt exactly the same way. And so the two fell asleep still embraced.

Oct. 7, 1957
Ashdod Harbor, Israel
Israeli Navy Base

FIVE DAYS LATER, David and Helga received the phone call that alerted them that they would be inserted into Egypt that night. David called the Mossad Headquarters and requested that a coded message be sent immediately to Abdul, alerting him to their impending arrival the following morning. He also requested that Abdul reach Alex and Omar and have them and their families be ready to be evacuated twenty-four hours later.

With that done, the two agents drove to the usual harbor in the evening and reported aboard the same MTB. Captain Levy welcomed them but was not his usual sardonic self. He evidently had been briefed on the upcoming operation and was concerned about his part in it.

Once the MTB had cleared the harbor, he sat down with the two agents and reviewed his part of the attack. He mentioned that twenty-four hours later, when the three Egyptian families were to be evacuated, he would send either two or three inflatables to the beach so that the three families could be safely removed before the attack began. He would then retreat back to Israel, leaving David and Helga to enter the labs as part of the strike force. The two would be evacuated from Egypt together with the strike force.

Once that was all made clear, Captain Levy went topside to conn the MTB on its trip to Egypt and its stealthy approach to the beach.

Oct. 8, 1957
Egyptian Shore

THE TWO AGENTS REMAINED below, waiting to be told it was time to board the usual inflatable. The agents heard the sound of the muffled engines die away and knew the time had come to disembark from the MTB. They went topside where Captain Levy approached them, and speaking very softly, said, "Listen, you two miserable clowns. I've gotten used to your ugly faces, so make damn sure you get back safely! And for God's sake, don't screw up like last time. It took my crew three hours to clean up David's blood."

Without another word, he embraced first Helga and then David, then turned away to oversee the launching of the inflatable and the boarding of the two crewmen and the two agents. As the crewmen prepared to begin paddling toward shore, the captain leaned over the side and whispered, "Good luck," and waved goodbye.

The two crewmen paddled silently toward shore until they were about a hundred yards out. Then they stopped and listened intently. Their previous trip had taught them to be extremely careful and be on the lookout for security patrols with dogs. The crewmen sat there and let the inflatable just drift as they listened intently. Finally, they began paddling again, but very slowly. Eventually, all on board could hear the sound of the very light surf, and shortly they grounded on the beach. David and Helga lost no time scrambling ashore, and the inflatable disappeared on its way back to the MTB.

David and Helga immediately began putting some distance between themselves and the beach. Their thinking was that any patrols were most likely to be along the beach and not further inland. After an hour of rapid hiking, they stopped and rested for a while. They did not want to reach the village and Abdul's house too early.

After a time, they resumed their hike but moved more slowly. Dawn found them quite close to the village. They sat down behind a small hill and waited patiently for people to start moving around in the village. Eventually, they felt it was safe to walk to Abdul's house. Both Abdul and his wife were there, and they greeted the agents with hugs.

Inside the house, David and Helga waited to hear if Abdul had been able to reach either Alex or Omar. Luckily, Abdul had been able to reach Omar, and now both he and Alex knew they had to come to Abdul's house that evening with their families.

David and Helga consumed a good breakfast prepared by Abdul's wife and then retired to the shed behind the house to rest for a number of hours. They knew that once night came, they would be very busy for a considerable number of hours.

Oct. 9, 1957
Abdul's House and the Labs

LATE IN THE EVENING, Alex, Omar, and their wives and children arrived at Abdul's house. Introductions were made all around, and then David said he had some instructions for all of them.

David said, "We are all going to leave here around 11 tonight. It will take three to four hours to reach the beach on foot and the pick-up point. I hope all the children can handle the hike. If not, Helga and I can help carry them. That won't be a problem. However, we all are going to have to be very quiet, especially the children. So I am going to ask the parents to take their children aside and impress them with the vital importance of not talking. If they do need to ask for anything, they need to whisper. Does everyone clearly understand that?"

There were nods all around.

David asked, "Are there any questions?"

There were none.

With an hour before they set off, everyone tried to relax and nap. When the time came to begin the trek to the beach, David and Helga gathered everyone, and in the dark they set off. David led the group. After thirty minutes, he stopped the group and suggested they sit down for a short rest. David and Helga were carrying large water canteens, and they made sure everyone drank. David also distributed some energy bars to the adults.

Then they set off again with David carrying a small child on his shoulders. Helga carried a two-year-old child on her shoulders. Throughout the next few hours, the same routine was repeated, and the group moved slowly yet steadily toward the rendezvous point at the beach.

By the time the group reached the beach, it was almost 4 a.m. As the group got closer to the beach, the adults listened intently for any sounds of security patrols and the dogs that always accompanied them. However, by some miracle, no patrols seemed to be in the vicinity.

David signaled the MRB lying offshore, and twenty minutes later, three inflatables appeared. David and Helga helped the three families to board the little craft. Then, with a wave, the three craft disappeared in the night, and David and Helga set off at a brisk pace to reach the location on the beach where the IDF brigade should already have landed. After an hour of steady and rapid walking, they were suddenly stopped by a voice coming out of the darkness and challenging them in Hebrew. Helga answered, and they were brought to the brigade command center. The commander welcomed them and suggested they sit or lie down in the sand and wait for daylight and the order to move in on the lab building. David and Helga lay down gratefully, using their backpacks as pillows. Around them, members of the troop brigade lay quietly, sometimes whispering to each other, and pretty soon David and Helga fell into a light slumber.

Oct. 10, 1957, 8:00 a.m.
Lab. Building, Egypt

David and Helga woke up when the soldiers around them began getting ready to move in on the lab Building. The two agents shouldered their backpacks and checked the revolvers they had been issued by the Mossad. An IDF Major came up to them and said, "If you two will please stay with me, we will enter the labs building together. I know your assignment is to help locate the three Nazi Colonels."

The Major moved off, and the two agents walked close behind him. Around them, the members of the brigade marched in a loose formation. David could hear the sound of aircraft in the distance, which he assumed were the jets from the U.S 6th Fleet, which were operating as a distraction of the Egyptian radar.

After an hour of marching, they could see the fake hosiery mill building in the distance. The brigade stopped and waited. A few minutes later, a much louder sound of aircraft engines was heard. A number of twin-engine transports appeared overhead, and numerous parachutes blossomed in the sky.

The paratroopers spread out as soon as they landed, and, moving swiftly, surrounded the building and sealed off all approaches to it. The entire IDF attack turned out to be a total surprise for both the Egyptian military and the lab security force. The Egyptian radar had been fooled by the aircraft of the U.S. 6th Fleet flying on daily maneuvers for a week, a few miles offshore. When the Israeli transports carrying the paratroops appeared on the screens of the Egyptian radar, they were simply thought to be more U.S. Navy aircraft launched from the U.S. 6th Fleet not far away.

The Major escorting David and Helga led them to what was an entrance to the building. Following the blueprint of the building that David had obtained from Alex, they located a stairway that led to the labs built below the fake ground-level building. There, they found the occupants in a state of panic and chaos. It was obvious that the IDF attack had come as a total and complete surprise. The IDF troops had already begun screening the employees of the labs. Those employees who were obviously ignorant of the true purpose of the labs were told to go home and did so without delay, happy to leave unharmed. Other employees were questioned more intensely, and a few were told they would be taken to Israel for further questioning. The screening process continued for some time until only a few employees were left in the underground labs.

The Major told David and Helga that a small number of personnel had retreated to a single lab and had barricaded themselves there. The IDF troops quickly overcame the minimal resistance the small group put up. The Major, together with David and Helga, entered the large lab room. Helga, who carried photos of the two Nazi scientists, quickly located them among the other personnel, and these two were taken out under heavy guard. Then Helga spotted Colonel Rochman, who had been trying to hide behind some other lab personnel. Before anyone could react, Rochman had stepped out, grabbed Helga, and was holding her in front of him as a shield with a pistol held against her head. Everyone in the room froze, afraid to panic Rochman into shooting Helga.

Suddenly, with absolutely no warning, Helga bent over just enough and kicked backward and upward, hitting Rochman in his groin. Rochman involuntarily spread his legs when he felt the pain from the kick. David saw his chance, whipped out his pistol, and shot the Nazi Colonel in his right thigh, which had become exposed when he spread his legs. With that double pain, Rochman let go of Helga, dropped his gun, and fell to the floor. Helga turned around, kicked Rochman once in the face as hard as she could, and then stepped back as some IDF troops crowded around the fallen Nazi. They bandaged his wounded thigh and then carried him out of the building.

After kicking Rochman, Helga just stood there, not moving as if in a trance. David rushed over to her, put his arms around her, and just held her. He could feel her shaking. He said and did nothing for a couple of minutes and finally led her gently out of the building. Around them, IDF troops, including some technicians, were removing documents, plus a cylinder full of poison gas and a cannon shell designed to deliver a tactical nuclear charge.

Outside, the IDF brigade was already preparing to retreat to the beach. An IDF helicopter suddenly arrived, and the three Nazi Colonels were hustled aboard to be taken to Israel. When the lab building had been totally evacuated, an IDF demolition team carrying large quantities of powerful explosives entered the building. They laid the explosives both in the labs and in the phony mill built above them. Then they retreated to a safe distance.

The explosive charges were triggered remotely, and with some very loud explosions, the entire structure collapsed on itself amid flames and a rising column of black smoke.

David and Helga hiked amidst the retreating brigade and ninety minutes later arrived at the beach. A large number of Israeli Navy vessels floated near the beach. The Major that had been their escort, and who had walked back to the beach with them, now said, "If you would please come with me, arrangements have been made for your return to Israel."

The Major led them to a particular spot on the beach, and sure enough, there was the inflatable with the two familiar crewmen waiting for them. The same MTB was waiting close to shore, and David and Helga lost no time climbing aboard. Captain Levy welcomed them. He hugged Helga and then David without saying a word and then led them below, pointed to a cot, and disappeared topside. Shortly, the MTB's engines could be heard, and the vessel began its trip to its home port of Ashdod. At the same time, David's ears picked up the sound of jet fighters overhead and guessed they were Israeli jet fighters sent to cover the retreat of the brigade.

Twenty minutes later, a crewman came below and offered the two agents some hot soup, which they accepted gratefully. Then, to David's surprise, Helga suggested they go topside for the rest of the trip back to Israel. The two sat down on the open deck with Helga leaning against David. She turned to him and whispered, "David, it's finally over, isn't it?"

David answered, "Yes, darling, it is really over. Now maybe we can think about the future!"

Once the MTB arrived back at Ashdod, the two agents thanked Captain Levy profusely for all of his great service, got into their car, and drove to their Mossad apartment. There, the phone rang shortly after they arrived, and Helga answered it.

It was Esther Epstein, and she said, "Oh, Helga, Manny called me to let me know that you and David were safely back. Are you both all right?"

Helga said, "Yes, we are both O.K., just pretty tired. David is still not up to his usual self, but he'll be all right. We sure were very glad to be back and safe!"

Esther said, "Manny and I were very worried. Now I know I can sleep well tonight. Helga, do you think you and David could come over for dinner tomorrow night?"

Helga said, "Let me ask David."

David said he'd be happy to go.

Helga told Esther they would love to come. Helga added she was very pleased at the invitation and looked forward to seeing them the next day.

That evening, after dinner, David and Helga went out for an evening stroll. Then they returned home and both fell into a very deep sleep.

11

Oct. 10, 1957
Cairo, Egypt
President Nasser's Villa

The President of Egypt was woken early that morning by a phone call from a senior aide who informed him of the attack on the labs building by the Israeli Defense Force. The caller further informed Nasser that the labs building had been totally destroyed and the three Nazi Colonels taken to Israel. This meant the 'Sword of Damocles' project was in effect terminated.

Nasser flew into a rage, threatening to execute some of his closest advisers for not protecting this project from the Israelis. Eventually, he calmed down enough to call for a meeting of his top staff. They were all unanimous in recommending that no further steps against Israel be taken at this time. After much discussion, Nasser very reluctantly agreed. However, he ordered that a fake story be widely disseminated that the fake hosiery mill had been destroyed by a fire of unknown origin and that it would not be rebuilt any time soon.

Nasser then sent messages to the leaders of Syria and Jordan explaining how Israeli agents had infiltrated the 'Sword of Damocles' project, followed by the assault by the IDF. He also mentioned that the presence of the U.S. 6th Fleet had further complicated matters. At the end of the messages, Nasser promised to find an opportunity to take revenge on Israel.

The messages to Syria and Jordan were kept secret. But the net result was that politically powerful people in Egypt began losing faith in Nasser.

12

Oct. 11, 1957
Jerusalem, Israel
The Epstein Residence

When David and Helga arrived at the Epstein home, it was Esther who answered the door. She gave each of them an extra-long hug as if to convey the message of how happy she was to see them safe after the attack on the labs. She had obviously been told of the raid by her husband, Manny. The three sat in the living room making small talk while waiting for Manny to arrive. He eventually got home, and just like his wife, he gave David and Helga a big hug. Then they all went to the dining room and sat down to dinner.

Esther asked if they were relieved that their mission in Egypt had finally ended. Helga answered and said, "For me, it's been a nightmare, and I feel that now I can think about the future. Before, I really couldn't. David has been absolutely great in being supportive. Thanks to him, I feel as if I've come back to life again."

David said nothing, just smiled at Helga,

Then Esther brought up the subject of their future.

She asked, "David and Helga, have you given any thought to what you would like to have happen in your lives from now on?"

Helga quickly answered and said, "David and I both feel we don't want to be involved in field work from now on. We also want to get married and start a family. That also means I would have to move to America. David thinks we both could probably work as analysts for the CIA."

Manny, who had been silent until now, jumped into the conversation.

He said, "You know, I think the Mossad could probably be persuaded to talk to the CIA about you two and make a strong pitch to have both of you become analysts at Langley!"

Helga said, "Manny, do you really think the Mossad would be willing to do that?"

Manny answered, "After what you did to destroy the 'Sword of Damocles' insanity, I believe it would not take much persuasion to have the Mossad put in a good word for both of you!"

David said, "Manny, that would really be greatly appreciated. Thank you!"

Now Esther brought up a subject close to her heart and said, "I hope you two haven't forgotten that Manny and I want to handle your wedding!"

David, speaking in a mock tone of surprise, said, "Wedding? I can't get married. I've got five girlfriends waiting for me back in Washington!"

Helga quickly said, "Esther, do you have a really big carving knife in your kitchen? I need it to do some major surgery on David!"

That brought a gale of laughter.

Then, after the laughter died down, Esther asked, "How would you two feel if I could arrange for your wedding three weeks from today?"

Helga looked at David with raised eyebrows, and he responded to the unspoken question by nodding yes.

Helga turned to Esther and said, "That would be great,

Esther. But please remember that neither David nor I wanted a big wedding."

Manny entered the discussion by saying, "I don't think you two realize how many people have heard about your part in this whole operation. There are quite a few people who are very grateful for what you two accomplished, and they might want to attend the wedding and participate in the happy event. So, Helga and David, you might want to keep that in mind."

Helga and David remained silent, not really sure of how to respond.

For the rest of the evening, Esther gently brought up various subjects relating to the forthcoming wedding, but the conversation was mainly with Helga, while Manny and David simply listened.

On the way home, Helga remarked to David, "You know, Esther is really into this wedding business. I don't think we should discourage her. I think it truly means a great deal to her to be able to organize our wedding as if we were family!"

David merely said, "Yes, that's pretty obvious. By all means, let her do this. It seems to me we are both very lucky to have friends like Manny and Esther!"

Oct. 15, 1957
Jerusalem, Israel
Prime Minister's Conference Room

The previous day, David and Helga had received a surprise phone call from the office of the Prime Minister politely requesting their presence the following day at 11 a.m. in the Prime Minister's conference room. The two agents did not know what to make of this invitation, but in any case arrived at the conference room a few minutes early, as was their custom.

There, they found Feingold, Manny Epstein, Colonel Levin

from the IDF, and two men from the Israeli Government who were not introduced. A few minutes later, the Prime Minister entered the conference room, welcomed everyone, and poured small cups of Demi tasse coffee for the attendees.

Then Ben Grunion looked directly at David and Helga and very politely asked if they minded being addressed by their first names. David looked at Helga, who simply smiled at him, and then said, "Of course not, Prime Minister."

Then Ben Gurion, still looking directly at the two agents, continued.

He said, "David and Helga, you were asked to be here today to receive the heartfelt thanks of the State of Israel. The two of you risked your lives repeatedly in order to penetrate this truly evil plan of Egyptian President Nasser. You were totally successful in helping defeat Nasser's plot and then even managed to render assistance to the IDF during the assault on the fake textile mill. Unfortunately, your exploits cannot be revealed to the general public for reasons of national security. Nevertheless, you both are receiving Israel's highest decoration for your gallant work!"

With that, Ben Gurion walked around the table and handed each agent a framed document while the others present all applauded vigorously.

David and Helga each thanked the Prime Minister profusely.

Ben Gurion sat down again and once more addressed the two agents directly.

With a twinkle in his eyes, he said, "Some of my super secret agents have informed me that the two of you have developed a romantic relationship! Good for you! I have also been told that once married, you want to live in the United States and that you no longer wish to continue doing field work. That makes perfect sense. But losing you, Cairo Rose, will be a serious loss for the Mossad and for Israel. Still, I'm sure it is for the best for you both. I just hope you will remember us in this tiny country and come and visit once in a while. I personally wanted to give you those awards and to wish you both happy and productive lives!"

With that, the few people in the room applauded again.

David looked at Helga and, with a motion of his hand, indicated she should respond for them both.

Helga stood up and addressed the Prime Minister directly.

She said, "Prime Minister, I know I speak for both David and myself when I say that it is truly an honor to receive these awards. Speaking for myself, Israel gave me refuge and a career just when I needed both desperately after the war. For that, I shall be eternally grateful. In addition, meeting and working with David changed my life and freed me from the horrors that I experienced at Treblinka. The Mossad became my home and my refuge for a number of years, but now I am ready to move on to the next phase of my life. Prime Minister, I hope you understand that I am not turning my back on Israel. But if David wants me to move to America, I believe that is the right move for me at this time."

Ben Gurion smiled kindly at Helga and said, "Helga, no one will ever think you are turning your back on us. You have been a true patriot, and we shall be in your debt forever. I agree with you that if moving to America to be with David is to be the next phase in your life, then I say more power to you. And know that you go with the blessing of Israel!"

Helga was so moved by the kind words of the Prime Minister that she choked up and could not say anything as tears wet her cheeks. David, seeing her reaction, quickly moved close to her and put his arms around her. No one said anything for a couple of minutes.

Then Colonel Levin, who had not said a word until then, suddenly spoke up.

He said, "Miss Horowitz and Mr. Knox, I feel you should

know that the building blueprints that you managed to spirit out of Egypt probably saved lives. And I also want you to know that you personally going into that building with the IDF troops, really energized them. They truly developed real respect for both of you!"

David felt he had to answer for both Helga and himself and said, "Colonel, if Helga and I helped in any minor way during the attack, you are most welcome. We two were most anxious to help destroy the 'Sword of Damocles' plot! Thank God it is exterminated!"

The Prime Minister chimed in with a heartfelt, "Amen to that!"

The meeting ended shortly thereafter. But before it ended, everyone present came up to David and Helga and shook their hand and congratulated them.

On the way back to their Mossad residence, David and Helga both felt that the Prime Minister had been extremely thoughtful to take the time to hold the meeting. Now they were both looking forward to their upcoming wedding.

Oct. 15- Nov. 6, 1957
Jerusalem, Israel
Various Places

OVER THE FOLLOWING DAYS, David and Helga were busy attending to various important and necessary items.

David took Helga to the U.S. Embassy and helped her fill out the necessary paperwork that would allow her to enter the U.S. as an immigrant.

David contacted his former handler at the CIA, Jack Riley, and informed him that he was going to be getting married in the next few days. He also advised Ridley that he and Helga both would be residing in the U.S. and that Helga might want to work for the CIA as an analyst. He pointed out that he wanted to retire from field work and wished to find a slot also as an analyzer.

Helga seemed to be very busy during this period, with numerous phone calls from Esther as well as meetings between the two. David decided the wisest thing he could do was to ask no questions and let Esther and Helga make all the necessary arrangements and decisions for the upcoming marriage.

By common consent between David and Helga, it had been decided that David should write a report detailing their activities during the last few days of the operation against the 'Sword of Damocles.' He discovered that writing such a report required a considerable amount of his time.

When David brought the report to the Mossad Headquarters, Feingold asked to see him. David went to Feingold's office, was welcomed, and asked to sit down.

Feingold said, "David, there have been a couple of things that I felt you and Helga should be told. First, through diplomatic channels, we have been told that President Nasser was so embarrassed by the failure of the 'Sword of Damocles' plot that he decided to not say a word about the incursion by the IDF and the destruction of the phony mill and the labs. He had a fence built around the site so as to keep people away because of the nuclear material and poison gas still present there. In time, Egypt will have to totally clean the site.

Second, the trials of the three Nazi Colonels are about to begin. Helga will be asked to give testimony in the trial of Colonel Rochman. I suspect that will be very traumatic for her. I hope you can help her get through this difficult period."

David answered, "Of course I will. I'll go to the trial every day with her and give her all the support I can!"

One day, there was a phone call from Abdul. He, Alex, Omar, and their three families had been granted asylum in Israel and were actively pursuing the required steps to enter the U.S as immigrants. The three families had been temporarily housed in Tel Aviv, and Abdul asked whether David and Helga could join them for dinner there one evening.

David and Helga were more than happy to drive to Tel Aviv and meet with the three families that they had helped rescue from Egypt. The meal turned out to be a happy occasion even though the three families were facing an uncertain future. But at least now they were no longer living in a country ruled by a dictatorship and could look forward to a much brighter future for themselves and their children.

So the three weeks passed more rapidly than either David or Helga had anticipated, and at the end of the three weeks, they only had to wait two days before their wedding would take place.

Nov. 8, 1957
Jerusalem, Israel
Beth Shalom Synagogue

On the day of their wedding, both David and Helga were somewhat nervous. It was certainly a novel experience for them both. Esther Epstein had found a simple yet beautiful dress for Helga and a very handsome suit for David.

At 10:30, a car and driver appeared at the Mossad residence to take the couple to the synagogue. Esther and Manny awaited them there, and Esther took charge of the nervous couple. Esther had located a liberal rabbi who was willing to perform a somewhat non-traditional Hebrew wedding with one of the couple being non-Jewish.

At the synagogue, Esther and Helga disappeared, and Manny took David to a waiting room. Then, at the appointed hour, Manny led David just outside the sanctuary. Then, as music sounded, Esther, as the maid of honor, entered the sanctuary and walked slowly and gracefully to stand before the rabbi on the left. David entered next, and walking somewhat more quickly, walked up the aisle to stand before the rabbi, but across from Esther. David was startled at how many people were seated in the sanctuary.

A minute later, Manny, with Helga on his left arm, entered the sanctuary. All eyes were on them as they walked slowly up the aisle.

Manny slowly led Helga to stand next to David. Then, as the best man, he moved to stand beside David.

When David turned to watch Manny and Helga walk up the aisle, he was shocked to see Prime Minister Ben Gurion sitting in the first row next to a very stately lady whom he assumed was his wife. Then David had no time to glance any further as Manny and Helga approached. Helga looked positively radiant as well as beautiful. The dress she wore set off her gorgeous figure to perfection. On his part, David gently but firmly took Helga's arm. He looked deep into her eyes for a second, smiled encouragingly, and then they both turned to face the rabbi.

The rabbi lost no time in beginning the wedding service. He spoke in a deep voice in English rather than Hebrew. As he spoke, it became obvious that he had been briefed on the background of both Helga and David. As the rabbi briefly mentioned the fact that Helga had lost her family in one of the Nazi execution camps, David felt Helga tighten her grip on his arm and felt her shaking slightly in an involuntary reaction to those past memories. David put a protective hand on the hand that Helga had put on his arm.

The rabbi continued the service. Then the synagogue's cantor, singing in a truly beautiful baritone voice, sang a Hebrew song that is typically performed at weddings. The rabbi then asked if this was a two-ring ceremony, and Manny answered yes.

Manny took two simple gold bands from his pocket and gave one to David and one to Helga. David then slipped the wedding band onto Helga's left hand, and Helga did the same to David with the band she was holding. Then the rabbi began speaking again and finally ended the service with a benediction, after which he suggested gently that David kiss his brand new bride.

David took her face in his two hands and kissed Helga gently and very lovingly. Then the couple walked back down the aisle, followed by the Epsteins, both of whom had big smiles on their faces. The attendees broke into spontaneous applause.

Outside of the sanctuary, a female employee of the temple led them to a large room that had been set up with a number of tables and a long buffet table loaded with food.

The employee showed that David and Helga were to stand with the Epsteins next to them to form a receiving line. A couple of minutes later, the first of the people who had attended the wedding began arriving. One of the first was Captain Levy, the MTB captain who had taken them on the numerous insertions into Egypt and then had returned them safely to Israel. He had a beautiful woman on his arm, obviously his wife, whom he introduced as Heather. After congratulating the couple, the captain, in a begging tone, said, "Would you please explain to my wife how I spent a number of nights getting you two in and out of Egypt!"

David, with a perfectly straight face, said, "Captain, what are you talking about? We were never in Egypt! And we certainly were never on your MTB!"

Helga added, "I certainly never saw you before!"

The captain's wife said, in a theatrical tone, "Darling, wait until I get you home."

Helga, unable to keep up the pretense, hid her face on David's shoulder and was silently laughing. Then David couldn't help laughing either. The captain said, "If I ever get you two on my MTB again, I may decide to dump you in the Mediterranean."

His wife, with an absolutely straight expression, said, "I guess now I know where you were all those nights! How am I going to explain all this to our eleven children!"

Captain Levy, caught off guard for a minute, said in a strange tone of voice, "What eleven children?"

His wife, David, and Helga all broke into uncontrolled laughter, joined by Captain Levy. They were all laughing so hard that tears were rolling down all of their cheeks, and people waiting in line to congratulate the couple wondered what had been said that was so funny.

Helga said, "Mrs. Levy, you said that so perfectly that you should have been an actress!"

Without batting an eye, Mrs. Levy answered, "I am an actress. I was in a couple of movies, but mostly I acted in the theater in both London and Israel."

Then the captain's wife, with a serious look on her face, said, "I truly hope you two will be as happy as Erik and I have been for many years!"

With that, she kissed first Helga and then David on the cheek, and the two moved on.

Colonel Levin, his wife, and their twenty-three-year-old son, a member of the IDF, came next.

Then Feingold and his wife came by, and they were followed by a familiar face. It was David's CIA handler, Jack Riley, who was alone. He congratulated the couple heartily. Right behind him was the Prime Minister and his wife. The Prime Minister, speaking very softly, said to David and Helga, "I want to personally tell you how grateful I and the entire Knesset are for your efforts in destroying the 'Sword of Damocles.' Know that Israel is forever indebted to you both."

With that, the Prime Minister and his wife moved on. Not

far behind him came Abdul, Alex, Omar, and their wives. David and Helga were truly happy to see them. Others came by and congratulated them. Finally, the line ended, and Esther suggested they go in and sample some of that good food before it all disappeared.

David and Helga went into the room where the food was and filled their plates. Then they looked around and saw that Esther had saved two seats for them at the head table. As they ate, various people came up to them and congratulated them.

After the guests had enough time to eat and drink, Esther Epstein stood up, approached a microphone that had been set up, and asked for everyone's attention.

She said, "Ladies and gentlemen, the time has come to give the newlyweds a rousing send-off with a wedding cake and champagne!"

With that, a huge round torte was brought out. Glasses and bottles of champagne were distributed. Then David and Helga were asked to come and stand before the torte. David was handed a huge, rather formidable-looking knife, and he was asked to begin cutting the torte. He looked at the knife, then the torte with such an expression of confusion that everyone burst out in a gale of laughter. Helga came to his rescue, and with her help, he began slicing the round torte as everyone applauded.

Then, to everyone's surprise, the Prime Minister himself approached the microphone. He cleared his throat and began speaking in a slow and deliberate manner.

"I do not know David and Helga hardly at all. But I know what they have accomplished to protect the State of Israel. May this marriage be blessed, and may their lives be rich and rewarding! L'chaim!"

With that, everyone present stood up and called out "L'chaim!"

The torte was distributed, the champagne poured, and the rabbi pronounced a blessing over David and Helga.

A small orchestra began playing Israeli folk dance tunes and other music. David led Helga to the dance floor, and as the orchestra played a waltz, they whirled around, accompanied by more applause. After a few seconds, Manny led Esther to the dance floor, and they joined the wedded couple. Soon, many people were dancing.

The dancing went on for some time. Eventually, the assembly of people began slowly dispersing, although many of those present came by and spoke to David and Helga once more. Among them were the Prime Minister and his wife, and the MTB captain and his wife.

When the MTB captain and his wife came by to say goodbye, she said, "David and Helga, I want to wish you a marriage that is as great as mine has been. I hope you two will have a great marriage, a productive life, and hopefully children before it's too late. God bless you both!"

With that, she kissed both David and Helga on the cheek, her husband, Captain Levy, shook their hands, and the two left the room.

Finally, the only guests left were the Prime Minister and his wife. They came over, and Ben Gurion said, "David and Helga, you will probably never know how important your efforts were in protecting the State of Israel. I believe I speak for everyone when I say thank you. My wife and I want to wish you both a wonderful life! Be well!"

With that, Ben Gurion embraced David and kissed Helga. His wife did the same, and the couple walked slowly out of the room.

Finally, only David and Helga were left in the room together with the Epsteins.

Helga, in a voice that trembled with emotion, said, "Esther

and Manny, I don't know how David and I can ever thank you enough for what you did! And Esther, you really did a magnificent job in organizing everything!"

David chimed in, "Yes, indeed! Without you two, we would simply have gone and gotten a civil wedding with no one around. Thank you so much!"

Esther was beaming as she said, "I think Manny and I were almost as excited about this wedding as you two were!"

And so the day ended, and David and Helga knew they would long remember their wedding day.

Nov. 14, 1957
Jerusalem, Israel
Federal Courthouse

THE TRIAL OF COLONEL ROCHMAN was held in a fairly large courtroom and was presided over by a panel of three Israeli judges. The entire trial was conducted in English and was recorded so that it could be reviewed by the War Crimes Tribunal at a later time. A jury was duly empaneled, and the trial began. Colonel Rochman was led in handcuffs. The prosecutor, an attorney with white hair, who spoke slowly and deliberatively, went through the list of crimes carried out by Rochman, all of which had been itemized after World War II by a War Crimes tribunal.

Then the prosecutor began calling witnesses, all of whom had been prisoners at the Treblinka Execution Camp. David and Helga attended the trial from the very first day.

For Helga, it was a painful process to attend the trial after the loss of her family and the raping performed on her by Rochman. There was no joy for her, just a process of cleaning out her painful memories and seeing retribution. She sat quietly through the first few days of the trial with David always sitting beside her.

Eventually, it was her turn to testify. She was sworn in, and the prosecutor asked her to describe her experience while a prisoner at the Treblinka Execution Camp.

Taking a deep breath, Helga, speaking slowly and very distinctly, began describing what it had been like for her at the Camp. She described seeing her family being taken away, and she also described the rape that Rochman had committed repeatedly until he was interrupted. Helga also described in some detail what life at the Camp had been like for her until she and others managed to escape. As she testified, tears began rolling down her cheeks. The head judge asked her if she wanted a recess, but she shook her head to indicate she did not want to stop her testimony.

Finally, the prosecutor was finished with his questions, and the defense attorney began grilling her. He had been brought in from Germany at Rochman's request. He was a middle-aged man who almost always spoke in a sarcastic manner.

He began his cross-examination of Helga by asking if she could provide any proof that she had been a prisoner at Treblinka during the war. By way of response, Helga pushed up the sleeve of her blouse that covered her left arm and showed him a number burned in her skin.

The chief judge interrupted the attorney and, addressing Helga directly, said in a gentle tone, "Miss Horowitz, we need all testimony to be verbal."

Helga answered, "Yes, your honor. I'll try to remember that."

Then, turning back to the defense attorney, she said, "Counselor, when each of us arrived at Treblinka and if we were not immediately designated to be executed, then we had an identifying number burned onto our upper left arm."

The defense attorney then asked, "Miss Horowitz, World War II was a long time ago. How do we know that your testimony regarding that period is correct?"

Helga first wiped her eyes before answering, then nailed the attorney with an absolutely direct and resolute look as she answered, "Counselor, when a person has seen their entire family taken away and executed, and when that same person had to submit to rape, one is unlikely to ever forget any of that for the rest of their life."

Defense counsel, seeing that this was not a productive line of questioning, moved on to other subjects. He repeatedly asked Helga whether she could be sure that Rochman was the man who had been in command of Treblinka. In response, Helga said, "Not only am I sure but I believe there are records from that time that show beyond any doubt that Colonel Rochman was the commander!"

As she said this, she looked directly at Rochman, who smirked at her.

The prosecutor asked permission of the head judge to ask some more questions. With permission granted, he turned to Helga and asked, "Miss Horowitz, in your opinion, was Colonel Rochman simply carrying out orders as he administered the execution of Jews and others at Treblinka during World War II?"

Helga thought about the question and then, again looking directly at Rochman, said, "Based on what I saw and experienced, I am convinced that Colonel Rochman is a sadist who truly enjoyed using torture on many of the prisoners!"

The defense attorney attempted to shake her testimony but was incapable of doing so.

Finally, the cross-examination was over, and Helga went back to her seat next to David. He put his arm around her and held her tightly without saying a word,

The head judge declared the proceedings over for that day, and David and Helga stood and began filing out behind many spectators. Suddenly, there in front of them stood Manny and Esther Epstein, who had evidently sat in the back of the courtroom. Esther impulsively embraced Helga and said, "Honey, I am so proud of you. You did a fabulous job! You made that defense attorney look like a jackass!"

Manny chimed in, "You really nailed Rochman to the wall! Great job!"

Then Esther said in a gentle tone, "Helga, if you and David are up to it, Manny and I would be honored to have you to dinner tonight?"

Helga looked at David, who simply said, "It's up to you, honey".

Helga hesitated briefly, thinking it over, and then said, "Esther, you always say the right thing. Thank you! Yes, it might be good for me and maybe David too to be with the closest friends we have in the world!"

Nov. 16, 1956
Jerusalem, Israel
The Epstein Residence

David and Helga went directly to the Epsteins' from the courthouse. Helga looked worn out, and Esther convinced her to lie down for a while in the guest room. While Helga napped and Esther began cooking dinner, David sat down with Manny.

Manny asked, "David, have you and Helga made any plans for your future?"

David hesitated, thinking about it. Finally, he said, "Manny, as I think I told you, both Helga and I want to get out of field work. And Helga agrees we should go to the U.S. as soon as possible. I think that if I talk to some of the people at the CIA, they might be willing to accept Helga as an employee. After all, she speaks Hebrew, Arabic, Polish, and English fluently. If nothing else, she could certainly be a translator,"

Manny said, "I agree. She would be great at that and maybe also as an analyst."

David said, "I have been thinking that possibly the CIA could use both of us as analysts."

Manny said, "I'm pretty sure I can persuade the Mossad to send the CIA a very strong recommendation together with a report showing how important your contributions have been in defeating the 'Sword of Damocles' project!"

David said, "Manny, I would really appreciate that! Thank you very much!"

Later that evening, during another of Esther's great dinners, Esther very gently brought up a different subject.

She asked, "Helga, have you and David thought about starting a family?"

Helga looked at David and then answered, "We really haven't. I'm not getting any younger, so if we are going to have children, this would be a good time. If we both get out of field work, then it would be a much better time to start a family. David, what do you think?"

David said, "I really haven't thought about being a father. Haven't had the time. But now that you bring up the subject, I feel that I might really like it. Helga, what do you think, should we have about a dozen children?"

Helga looked shocked, and then, realizing David had been joking, said, "David! Bite your tongue. It's me who has to have the children, not you!"

That brought loud laughter from Manny and Esther.

Nothing more was said about the matter that evening, but Esther had managed to lay the foundation for David and Helga to seriously think about having children.

Then Manny turned serious and brought up another, although related matter.

He said, "David, I have a bit of a surprise for you. For some reason, I really don't know what, I became curious about your family's ancestry. I knew that your maternal grandparents brought you up after your parents were killed because you once told me. So I became curious and reached out to someone I know at the CIA. I asked that individual if the CIA had any information about your grandparents. They did some research and discovered something very interesting. It seems your grandmother was Jewish, and so was your mother. So that actually makes you Jewish also. Small world, isn't it?"

David had a very surprised look on his face, and all he said was, "I'll be dammed!"

Esther chimed in and said, "I certainly hope not!"

This brought the house down as everyone laughed heartily.

Then Esther added, "Well, David, welcome to the wandering tribe!"

There was more laughter, and then Helga got up, walked over to David, and kissed him tenderly.

Manny and Esther just sat there and applauded.

Nov. 21, 1957
Jerusalem, Israel
Execution Yard

THE SEPARATE TRIALS of the three Nazi Colonels had been held concurrently and had ended within a few days of each other. The proof that was submitted in all three cases was so overwhelming that the defense attorneys for all three did not have much chance to defend their clients. The best they could hope to accomplish was to have their clients avoid death sentences. But that was not to be the case. All three juries rendered decisions that the Nazi Colonels should be executed by hanging. All appeals were turned down.

The day set for the executions dawned cold and cloudy

with a blustery wind. The media was not allowed to attend. Only a few officials were present. The Israeli Government had, however, decided to film the executions as proof that they had indeed taken place. The film was later sent to the World Court.

Three gallows had been erected in an enclosed courtyard that was part of the Federal Prison in Jerusalem. The three executions were to be carried out simultaneously.

The three Colonels were led out to the courtyard wearing only their prison uniform. Their hands were handcuffed behind their backs. They were shivering from the cold wind and from fear.

There was no bluster or bravado from any of them. They all realized this was the end of the line and that shortly they would be dead. Even Rochman, normally the one with the loudest voice, was silent.

The three Colonels were each led to their individual gallows. They were assisted up the steps to the platforms.

Then each Colonel in turn was asked if he had any last words they wanted to say. None did.

A rabbi brought in for the express purpose intoned a final blessing. Then black hoods were placed on the heads of each Nazi. Next, the hanging nooses were placed around their necks and made snug. Then the guards assisting in the executions came down from the three gallows and each went to stand by the lever that would release the trap door on that particular gallows.

An Israeli IDF General then gave the command, "Ready!"

A few seconds elapsed, then the General called out. "Execute!"

The three prison guards all pulled their levers simultaneously, and the three bodies fell through the trap doors and hung below, swinging gently.

A few minutes elapsed, and finally the three bodies were

lowered to the ground. A physician brought in for just this purpose checked each body to make sure all three were indeed dead. They were.

That ended the executions. Later that day, the bodies of the three Colonels would be cremated, a fitting end for these war criminals.

The government officials all dispersed without any pleasantries being exchanged. None of them had enjoyed being present at the executions. It was simply a duty that had to be carried out.

Later that day, the news of the executions became official. David and Helga were in their apartment when they heard the news on TV. Helga began softly crying, and David went to sit by her and held her for a long time, hoping to provide some level of comfort.

Finally, Helga stopped sobbing, dried her eyes, and turned to David.

She asked, "David, is it really over?"

David quietly answered, "Yes, darling, it is over. Now we can get on with the rest of our lives."

Epilogue

Nov. 1, 1962
Northern Virginia, USA
Home of David and Helga Knox

SIX YEARS HAVE PASSED SINCE THE END OF THE 'SWORD OF Damocles' nightmare.

David and Helga had moved to the U.S. David still worked for the CIA, but at his request, no longer in the field. Now he was an analyst.

Helga, as David's wife, agreed to move to the U.S. permanently. She applied for U.S. citizenship and, after waiting the compulsory five years, became a U.S. citizen.

Helga, with the assistance of the Israeli Mossad, was hired by the CIA, also as an analyst.

After moving to the U.S., David and Helga purchased a three-acre home site not far from Langley, Virginia, where the CIA Headquarters is located.

David retained an architect, and he and Helga, working with the architect, designed a very comfortable four-bedroom bungalow. A swimming pool attached to the house was included. The swimming pool was designed to be enclosed by a sliding roof so that it could be used year-round. A combination car garage, workshop, and storage area was built that was also attached to the house.

The site had large shade trees and was close to the Potomac River. There, David had a boathouse erected, and he purchased a small cabin cruiser. The site where they lived was also the home of various small animals, and occasionally, even a deer or two would come by.

There was a general aviation airport not very far away, and David periodically rented a small airplane and flew around for a couple of hours, thus maintaining his flying proficiency.

Not long after getting married, Helga became pregnant. Then, three years later, she became pregnant again. The older child, a girl, was named Esther after Esther Epstein. The second child, a boy, was named Eric.

David and Helga led busy, active lives. They became friendly with some of their neighbors as well as some of their co-workers at the CIA.

Every six months or so, Esther and Manny Epstein flew over from Israel and spent a couple of weeks as guests of David and Helga. Esther doted on the two Knox children, and they, in turn, looked at the Epsteins as their grandparents.

Once each year, the entire Knox family flew to Israel and stayed at the Epstein residence.

During the October Missile Crisis, both David and Helga became extremely busy assisting in the analysis of what the intentions of the Soviet Union really were.

Occasionally, David and Helga reminisced about their time together working to defeat the 'Sword of Damocles' plot. But that didn't happen very often. They concentrated on bringing up their children, on their work at the CIA, and on their friends. Their life was very rich and rewarding. David and Helga love and respect each other just as much as the day they got married. They have as much love and respect for their children. They spent time with their children and consider themselves very fortunate to have two lovely, intelligent, and healthy children.

Helga no longer thinks about the terrible time at the Treblinka Execution Camp. Thanks to the life she leads, she has been able to get beyond that terrible time in her life. Cairo Rose is no more. Instead, there is a family of four leading a rich and rewarding life.

Claude G. Luisada is a native of Italy. He emigrated to the US at the age of seven. Over the years he lived in Boston, Chicago, and Albuquerque, New Mexico, and now resides in Aiken, South Carolina. He worked in construction management, fixed asset inventory systems, construction project cost forecasting, and helped open a large medical center. *Cairo Rose and the Sword of Damocles* is Mr. Luisada's first novel.

www.ingramcontent.com/pod-product-compliance
Lightning Source LLC
LaVergne TN
LVHW010655110826
845149LV00014B/3111
9781968548063